Christmas in Michigan: Tales & Recipes

DISCARD

ed by Carole Eberly

eberly press
1004 Michigan Ave.
E. Lansing, MI 48823

To Bill, with love & fond Christmas memories

The real Santa Claus visited with children on the 12th floor of Hudson's in the 1940s.

Although I have chosen old recipes from Michigan cookbooks for this collection, they are still workable today. However, at times you will have to use your common sense when they call for such things as "bake in a moderate oven until brown." I purposely did not make these recipes as specific as the ones we use today, mainly to preserve the flavor of how our mothers and grandmothers put together holiday feasts and other meals.

Such comments as "add ten cents worth of walnut meats" were too charming to be left out. Again, common sense is called for, since ten cents worth of walnut meats today is likely to net you a thimbleful of walnut dust.

A few recipes left me completely bewildered. For instance here is a recipe for:

Jumbles

One cup butter, two cups sugar, four eggs, four cups flour, one teaspoon soda. Use a jumble machine.

What is a jumble machine?
Have fun.

—Carole Eberly

Table of Contents

Table of Contents

Mom's Christmas Started After Labor Day

By Robert Clock

Although my mother was skilled in the domestic arts and could have staged a first-rate Christmas celebration with one arm in a cast, she always insisted that the whole family pitch in to help. And for Agnes Clock, Christmas preparations usually started the day after Labor Day.

"Remember to meet me at the streetcar stop," she would remind me as I ate breakfast the first day of school. "Hudson's is having a sale and I want to look at camisoles for Aunt Sally. If we don't start our Christmas shopping now, we'll never get it done."

Of course, I never had to be reminded twice about an impending trip to downtown Detroit. I loved riding streetcars and once we hit Woodward Avenue I could usually wheedle a hot fudge sundae out of my mother at the Fred Sanders store.

I am sure she could have shopped without me, but I learned quite a bit standing at her elbow about the merits of sterling over silverplate, why china lasts longer than ordinary crockery and how to separate real value from pure junk in the toy department.

On one of her early shopping expeditions she would usually pick out her Christmas cards — never less than 200 and no two alike. Furthermore, she refused to have them imprinted with her name.

"Sending a Christmas card with your name printed on it is worse than writing a letter to a close friend on a typewriter," mother decreed. She left the impression that she was well acquainted with any number of scoundrels who wrote personal letters on typewriters and sent imprinted Christmas cards who were now roasting in etiquette hell.

She refused help on addressing her Christmas card envelopes because none of us kids could even come close to her flowery Palmer Method script, but she always needed one of us close at hand to help decide which card should be sent to whom. Her cards always had to match some personal peculiarity of the recipient.

Tipplers on her list invariably received cards depicting a half dozen inebriated gentlemen in greatcoats and long mufflers stumbling out of a horse-drawn coach in front of a heavily-timbered wayside inn in Merry Olde England.

If you recently moved to the suburbs, you could expect to find a picture of a mailbox jammed with gaily decorated packages on your Christmas card. If you lived in the country, your greeting would feature a snow-whitened landscape with a sleigh in the foreground heading for a distant farmhouse with a wreath of woodsmoke curling from the chimney.

"The Wilsons just got a dog," mother would say. "Find me one with a dog on it."

"We don't have any dogs," I would answer, shuffling through the cards. "But I can give you a camel, two sheep, or a jackass."

"Give me the sheep. They look a lot like dogs. Besides, Maud's eyes are going and she won't be able to tell the difference. We'll save the jackass for Uncle Harry."

Preachers, Sunday School teachers and their ilk always received cards heavily laced with Christmas Scripture; choir directors would receive pictures of heavenly angels singing "O Holy Night;" merchants and sales clerks were assigned old-fashioned street scenes; and the totally irreverent were mailed cards depicting rowdy snowmen or frolicking reindeer.

I don't know if the recipients of mother's cards ever realized the labor that went into their selection, but the annual ritual was tantamount to a university course in human relationships.

Mother usually tried to have most of her shopping done by the middle of November, giving us almost six weeks to get the house ready for the holiday season. Walls had to be washed, wallpaper cleaned with balls of a soft, dough-like substance called Climax, draperies dry-cleaned, curtains washed and stretched, floors polished and rugs beaten until they cried for help.

Of course, mother insisted that we all work right along with her so that she would get done in time to make springerles and pfeffernusse, which also demanded our presence in the kitchen. She had a very generous sampling policy, however, so none of us minded.

When we weren't busy at manual labor, mother had us ringed around the dining room table learning the proper way to wrap packages. She taught us always to cushion drygoods in tissue paper, to fold wrapping paper over a table knife to insure sharp corners and to rub the streamers on bows between your thumbs and a scissors' blade to make the curl.

Early in December mother began making a list of all of the "feather parties" scheduled by church groups throughout the inner city. For the uninitiated, "feather parties" were no more than old-fashioned Bingo games, but the prizes were live poultry which you were supposed to take home and fatten up for Christmas dinner. The first prize was always a big tom turkey.

For some reason, "feather parties" were held in the basements or parish halls of obscure churches on the East Side of Detroit, involving long trips by streetcar with multiple transfers. Mother usually invited me to tag along, not to play but to help bring home the booty.

Her luck was phenomenal, and we seldom returned without a fat chicken or a brace of ducks in a wooden crate sharing our seat on the streetcar. But she never won a turkey, which was our traditional Christmas entree.

This meant that mother would have to deal with neighborhood poulterers, none of whom had her complete trust. She would not, under any circumstance, purchase a turkey that had been kept in cold storage more than a few hours. She never even considered the awful possibility of preparing, roasting, and consuming a turkey that had actually been frozen.

I can see her now, standing in front of a display case of iced toms at the butcher shop.

"Let me have a look at that fellow," she'd say, pointing to a deceased gobbler reclining on a bed of chipped ice. "How long has he been dead?"

"I killed him myself this morning, m'am," the butcher would say, holding up the bird — still equipped with head and feet — for my mother's inspection.

"He hasn't been in cold storage then?" she would press on, jabbing the bird's breast with a gloved finger.

"No, m'am. The carcass is scarcely cold."

"He looks like he was killed at Gettysburg," my mother would say, shaking her head. "But I guess he will have to do. You can cut off the head and feet before you weigh him."

On Christmas Eve after the tree was up and decorated and the latest Christmas cards had been added to the display over the archway, several major chores still remained: polishing the silverware and candlestick holders until they shone like the Christmas star; pressing the over-sized white linen tablecloth; glazing cranberries in sugar over low heat until they looked like crushed rubies; cleaning a mountain of shrimp for dipping; stuffing dates with walnut halves and rolling them in powdered sugar; assembling the turkey dressing so it would be ready the first thing the next morning.

Although mother always made the dressing herself, she needed someone to stand by to sample it as one ingredient after another went into her largest mixing bowl. When we kids declared that her raw stuffing had reached a new state of perfection, she would sample it herself.

"There's probably too much sage to suit your grandmother, but it tastes fine to me." Then she would wrap the bowl in a tea towel and put it on the back porch table next to the turkey. The ice box was never big enough to hold all of the good things she had prepared.

Then suddenly one crisp fall day in 1964 mother was gone and none of us thought the holidays would ever be the same again. That first Christmas my wife Judy and I invited the family to our new home in Holly, hoping somehow that a change of scenery would take the sting from our first Christmas without her.

Before our guests arrived, I walked through the house which was still faintly redolent of Spic 'n Span and Murphy Oil Soap. The Christmas tree, surrounded by packages with sharp edges and curly bows, was ablaze in the living room. Nearby on a coffee table were plates of chilled shrimp, stuffed dates, springerles and pfeffernusse. Christmas cards were strung across the entrance to the dining room where silverware gleamed on snowy linen. A crystal bowl of cranberries in the middle of the table glowed like crushed rubies in the candlelight. From the kitchen came the aroma of roast turkey and sage dressing.

Outside I heard a car door slam and the sound of familiar voices — and familiar laughter — on the front walk. For the first time I realized that mother hadn't left at all.

11

Michigan State Federation of Women's Club Cookbook, 1909

Delicate Indian Pudding

One qt. milk, 2 tablespoons yellow Indian meal, 4 tablespoons sugar, 1 tablespoon butter, 2 eggs, 1 teaspoon salt. Boil milk in double boiler, sprinkle in the meal stirring all the while. Cook 12 minutes stirring often. Beat together the eggs, salt and sugar and ½ teaspoon ginger. Stir the butter into the meal and milk. Pour this gradually over the egg mixture. Bake slowly 3/4 hour. Serve with sauce of heated syrup and butter.

*

Christmas Plum Pudding

Soak 1 lb. stale bread crumbs in 1 pt. hot milk. When cold, add to it ¹/₂ lb. sugar and the yolks of 8 eggs beaten to a cream. 1 lb. seeded raisins floured, 1 lb. currants washed, dried and floured, ¹/₄ lb. citron cut in slices and floured. 1 lb. beef suet chopped finely and salted, 1 glass wine, 1 glass brandy, 1 nutmeg and a tablespoonful of mace, cloves and cinnamon mixed. Beat the whole well together and the last thing add 8 beaten whites. Steam 6 hours. This is best made a week before using and warmed up in a steamer.

*

Pudding Sauce

One cup pulverized sugar, 1 cup cream, ¹/₃ cup butter. Cream the butter and sugar, add 1 egg beaten thoroughly to the butter and sugar. then whip the cream and put all together. Flavor with vanilla.

*

Food for the Gods

Whites of 6 eggs beaten stiff, 2 cups sugar, 6 tablespoons cracker crumbs, 2 teaspoons baking powder, 1 cup chopped English walnuts, 1 cup cut dates. Bake in slow oven 1 1/2 hour. Serve with whipped cream.

*

Marshmallow Cream

Take 1/2 lb. marshmallows, cut them up into quarters and pour over them 1 pt. cream. Let stand 3 hours. Stir once in awhile. When ready to serve put into it sliced pineapple and nut meats. Keep in a cold place.

*

Dessert

Put in sherbet glasses enough fruit (any kind or kinds desired, fresh or canned) with nuts to half fill glasses. Make a jelly by boiling 1 cup maple syrup and 1 cup water. Thicken with cornstarch and pour over fruit, filling glasses about 3/4 full. Cover with whipped cream and serve.

*

Waffles

Two cups flour, 1 1/2 cups milk, 2 level teaspoons baking powder, 2 tablespoons melted butter, 2 eggs, 1/2 teaspoon salt. Sift flour, baking powder and salt together. Beat yolks of eggs, add to milk, stir into flour, beating thoroughly. Then add melted butter and lastly the stiffly beaten whites of eggs. Bake in hot, well-greased waffle irons. Serve with maple syrup or honey.

*

Oatmeal Cookies

One cup white sugar, 3/4 cup lard, 2 well beaten eggs, 3/4 teaspoon soda, 2 scant cups flour, 2 scant cups rolled oats, 1 teaspoon cinnamon, 3/4 cups chopped raisins, 2 tablespoons sweet milk. Bake in moderate oven.

*

Maple Mousse

Two cups maple syrup, yolks of 4 eggs, put in double boiler and stir constantly until done. Stir while cooling. When cold, add 1 pt. whipped cream, pack in ice and salt for 5 hours before using. This serves 8 persons.

*

Penoche

Two and one-half cups brown sugar, 1/2 cup cream, butter size of an eggs. Boil until it will form a ball in cold water. Add 1/2 cup chopped walnuts, 1/2 cup chopped almonds, 1 teaspoon vanilla. Beat well and pour into buttered tins. Cut in squares before cool.

*

Burnt Cream

One qt. milk, 4 tablespoons cornstarch, 1 1/4 lbs. brown sugar, 1/2 cup walnuts. Put milk to boil, when hot add cornstarch blended with a little cold milk, stir till it thickens. Burn the sugar in an iron pan until it is deep brown, pour into the cornstarch, add the walnuts broken up. Pour into a mould and set away to chill. Serve with cream.

*

Pumpkin Pie

One cup milk, 1 cup pumpkin, ½ cup sugar, 2 tablespoons molasses, 2 tablespoons melted butter, 1 tablespoon ginger, 2 eggs slightly beaten, 1 teaspoon cinnamon, ½ teaspoon salt.

*

Christmas Sweetmeat

Grind through meat chopper 1 lb. each of dates, figs and raisins and ten cents worth of walnut meats. Mix all together with powdered sugar until it forms a stiff loaf. Roll into a sheet using the sugar liberally on the kneading board. Cut in little shapes and roll in granulated sugar. Place on platters to dry. Will keep well.

*

Peterboro Candy

Place 2 lbs. sugar, $^1/_2$ cup water, $^1/_4$ lb. butter and 1 can condensed milk in saucepan over moderate fire and stir for forty minutes. Remove from fire, add 1 teaspoon each of vanilla and lemon extract. Turn into oiled pans and when cool, cut into neat squares.

*

Huckleberry Cake

One cup sugar, 1 cup sour milk, 1 egg, 3 cups flour — full measure, 3 tablespoons melted butter, 1 teaspoon soda, $^1/_2$ teaspoon salt, 1 pt. berries floured and lightly stirred in. Bake 40 minutes.

*

Delicious Fruit Cake

Four cups sifted flour, 3 cups granulated sugar, 2 cups butter, 8 eggs, 2 pounds raisins, chopped, 2 pounds currants, washed and dried, 1/2 pound citron, cut in thin slices, 1/4 teaspoon nutmeg, 1 teaspoon salt, 1 teaspoon each of cloves, cinnamon, allspice and soda.

Cream sugar and butter; add yolks of eggs well beaten, then spices, then flour in which soda has been well sifted; next add whites of eggs, beaten to a stiff froth, and lastly, the fruit well dredged with flour. Line tins with two thicknesses of well buttered paper, fill about half full with the cake batter, and bake in a slow oven about 3 hours. As the top of cake browns, cover with paper to prevent burning.

*

Doughnuts

One and one-half cups flour, 4 teaspoons baking powder, 1 teaspoon each salt and cinnamon. Sift all together. Two eggs, 1 cup sugar, 6 tablespoons melted butter, 2 cups milk and 1 tablespoon over. Beat eggs until very light, slowly add sugar beating all the time and the melted butter. Beat all together into the prepared flour, add the milk and enough flour to roll out. Make into figure 8's and fry in deep lard.

*

Christmas shoppers jam Detroit's Woodward Avenue in the 1920s.

Kartoffel Torte (German Potato Cake)

Pass through a ricer or sieve enough cold boiled potatoes to make 2 cupsful. Chop fine enough blanched almonds to make 1 cup. Sift together 3 times; 2 cups of flour, 2 level teaspoons baking powder, 1 scant teaspoon salt, 1 teaspoon cinnamon, 1/2 teaspoon cloves. Cream 1 cup butter and gradually beat in 2 cups sugar and 1 cup sweet chocolate grated. Then add the beaten yolks of 4 eggs, 3/4 cup milk, the potatoes, flour and almonds, and lastly the beaten whites of the 4 eggs. Bake in large tube cake pan, in moderate oven for 1 hour. When cold, cover with chocolate icing.

*

Hermits

One and one-half cups brown sugar, 1 cup butter, 3 eggs, 1/2 cup sweet milk, 1 teaspoon baking powder, 3 cups flour, 1/2 teaspoon soda dissolved in 1/4 cup of hot water, 1 lb. raisins, 1 cup walnuts, 1 teaspoon each cinnamon, cloves, a little grated nutmeg. Drop a teaspoonful on buttered tins and bake in a moderate oven.

*

Banbury Tart

One-fourth lb. figs, 1 cup seeded raisins, 1 cup water, 1½ cups sugar, 1 orange, rind and juice, 1 lemon, rind and juice, 1 cup nutmeats. Chop fine figs, raisins, rinds and nutmeats, cook all until thick, then let cool. It is better if made the day before using. Roll rich pie crust thin and cut with biscuit cutter. Place 1 tablespoon of mixture on one side of the crust, fold over, bake a light brown and roll in powdered sugar.

Delicious to serve with coffee.

*

Red Currant Relish

The juice from 5 lbs. red currants, 5 lbs. sugar, 2 lbs. seeded raisins chopped fine, 5 oranges cut into dice including the rind. Cook all together for 25 minutes. Put into jelly glasses and when cold, cover with parafin.

*

Boiled Salad Dressing

One egg or the yolks of 2, 3 tablespoons melted butter or salad oil, 6 tablespoons good vinegar, 1 tablespoon sugar, ½ teaspoon dry mustard, 1 level teaspoon salt. Cook in double boiler until thick, when cold add, after whipping, a scant half cup of sweet cream.

*

Cream Tomato Soup

Cook 1 cup tomato and 1 cup water and rub through a sieve to remove seeds. Thicken with 1 teaspoon flour and season with salt, pepper and butter. Add soda size of a small pea. Just before serving add 1 cup milk previously heated.

*

Creamed Oysters

One large tablespoon butter, when it is melted add 1 table-poon flour, stir until it thickens, then add 1 cup cream, season with salt and pepper to taste, add the oysters drained and cook until the oysters are plump. Use as many oysters as the amount of sauce will warrant. Serve as cooked or on hot toast.

*

Oyster Cocktail

Place small oysters on ice until needed. Have glasses in which they are to be served chilled also. Make sauce of 2 tablespoons tomato catsup, 12 drops tobasco sauce and 1 teaspoon pepper sauce, juice of 1 lemon, 1/2 teaspoon grated horseradish, little salt and paprika. Add 2 tablespoons oyster liquor. Mix thoroughly and set on ice to chill. Put 5 oysters in each glass, pour sauce over and serve at once.

*

Waldorf Salad

Six good sized apples, 6 bananas, 2 stalks celery, 1 cup English walnut meats. All this is to be diced fine.

Dressing — Four tablespoons sugar, 1/2 teaspoon salt, 1/2 teaspoon cornstarch or flour, 1 teaspoon dry mustard, pinch of red pepper, 1 egg, 1/2 cup vinegar, piece of butter half as large as an egg. Cook until it creams. When cold, add 1/4 (generous) pt. sweet cream whipped stiff.

*

Fruit Salad

Apples diced, pineapple, celery, dates and walnut meats.

Dressing — 1 egg, 1 teaspoon salt, 1 tablespoon sugar, 1 teaspoon mustard, 1 teaspoon flour, a pinch of red pepper, 1/2 cup sweet milk, butter size of a walnut, 1/2 cup vinegar. Cook and thin with cream.

*

Street decorations at night on Woodward Avenue in Detroit.

Razzle Dazzle

Two qts. cherries, pitted, 2 qts. currants, 2 qts. red raspberries, 1 qt. green gooseberries. Put gooseberries at the bottom of the kettle, cherries next, currants next, red raspberries on top; to every pound of fruit add 3/4 lb. of granulated sugar. Boil until it jellies.

*

Orange Marmalade

Seven fine oranges, 2 lemons, cut off thick skin at ends and slice lengthwise into 8 pieces, then slice again very thin removing all seeds. To each pound of fruit add 1 qt. of water and set away for 24 hours. Then boil the fruit until tender (about 1 hour) and set away 24 hours. Third morning, to each pound add 1 lb. of sugar and boil until the juice jellies (about 3/4 of an hour). Put in glasses and seal when cool.

This recipe book took first prize at the World's Fair in Chicago.

*

Heavenly Hash

Five lbs. red currants or cherries, 5 lbs. granulated sugar, 3 oranges cut in small pieces, 1 orange rind shredded, 2 lbs. seeded raisins, 1 lb. figs. Put all ingredients into a granite kettle and boil until thick, stirring often. When done put into jelly cups or cans.

This is delicious and will keep indefinitely.

*

Malaga Grape Salad

One lb. of Malaga grapes cut open and seeded, 1 apple cut in small dice, 1 small stalk of celery cut up, 1/4 lb. English walnut meats. Mix together 1/2 pt. cream whipped very stiff, 1 tablespoon mayonnaise dressing and 1/4 cup sugar. Mix lightly with fruit when ready to serve and serve on lettuce leaf.

*

Tomato Gelatin

A tomato jelly which is delicious served with a green salad and mayonnaise dressing as made as follow:

Boil 1 qt. of canned tomatoes 20 minutes with 1 bay leaf, 6 cloves, 6 peppercorns, 1 spring parsley, and 1 slice of onion. At the end of that time strain the tomatoes through a sieve, return the liquid to a kettle and add 2 tablespoons tarragon vinegar, 2 tablespoons gelatine which has been softened in cold water, and salt to taste. Stir until the gelatine is dissolved and turn into a mold. When it is firm and ready for use, turn into a bed of crisp lettuce and water cress and pour over it a mayonnaise dressing.

*

Cucumber Sauce

Beat $1/2$ cup heavy cream stiff, add salt and a few grains of cayenne to taste and gradually 2 tablespoons vinegar. Then add 1 medium cucumber pared, chopped and drained and sufficient onion juice to flavor delicately.

*

Cream of Mushroom Soup

One-half lb. mushrooms, 4 cups chicken, 1 small onion sliced, 1/4 cup butter, 1/4 cup flour, 1 cup cream, salt and pepper. Chop mushrooms, add to the stock with the onion and cook 20 minutes, then rub through sieve. Return the above to the range, bind with butter and flour cooked together, pepper and salt to taste. Add cream last with a spoonful of whipped cream for each person at time of serving.

*

Cheese Balls

Mix 1 1/2 cups grated mild cheese with 1 tablespoon flour, 1/4 teaspoon salt, a few grains cayenne, and the beaten whites of 3 eggs. Shape in small balls, roll in cracker dust, fry in deep fat, and drain on brown paper.

*

Use your own (or somebody's else) worn out automobile batteries for the doorbell current.

Santa in a museum display at Michigan State University.

Turkey Bone Soup

After a roasted turkey has been served, use the skeleton for the soup. Cut off carefully a cupful of the meat, and reserve for force meat balls. Break the bones apart and with the stuffing still adhering to them, put into a kettle with 2 qts. of water, 1 tablespoon salt, a pod of red pepper broken in pieces, 3 or 4 blades of celery cut into inch pieces, 3 medium sized potatoes and 2 onions all sliced. Let boil slowly but constantly 4 or 5 hours. After half an hour before dinner, lift bones, skim off fat, strain through colander, return to soup kettle. (To remove fat from soups, pieces of writing paper laid upon it an instant will absorb it.) There will now be little more than a quart of soup. If more is desired, add a pint of hot milk or milk and cream, or a little water.

For the force meat balls, chop the scraps of turkey very fine, take $1/2$ teaspoon cracker crumbs smoothly rolled, a salt spoon of salt, a little cayenne pepper, a little grated lemon peel and $1/2$ teaspoon powdered summer savory or thyme, mix these together and add a raw beaten egg to bind them. Roll the mixture into balls the size of a hickory nut and drop into the soup ten minutes before serving.

*

Escalloped Potatoes

Slice potatoes very thin, butter baking dish, put in potatoes, seasoning with pepper, salt and bits of butter, put a layer of cracker crumbs on top, with bits of butter, pour over this a cream dressing. Bake 3/4 hour.

*

Potato Croquettes

One and $1/2$ pts. cold mashed potatoes, mix lightly with the well beaten whites of 2 eggs, make into balls and roll in beaten yolks of eggs, and then in bread crumbs. Fry in wire basket in hot lard.

*

❖❖❖

Things that may be eaten with the fingers — olives, which should never be handled with a fork; asparagus, when served whole; lettuce, which can be thus dipped in the dressing; celery, which may properly be placed on the tablecloth beside the plate; strawberries, when served with the stems on; fruits, cheese, potato chips, bread, toast, tarts, small cakes.

Steamed Squash in the Shell

Cut off the top of a Hubbard squash and steam till tender, scoop out pulp, mash and pass it through a vegetable sieve. Season with salt, pepper and butter and add 1 tablespoon cream and the beaten white of an egg. Return to the shell and score the top with a knife, place in a moderate oven to reheat twenty minutes before serving.

*

Potato Puffs

Two mashed potatoes beaten light; add 2 tablespoons melted butter; 2 well beaten eggs, a cup milk and a little salt. Put in deep dish and bake in oven.

*

Escalloped Tomatoes

Line a deep dish with bread spread with butter, slice tomatoes, seasoning with salt, pepper and butter. Put a middle layer of bread and butter. Fill dish with tomatoes, placing over the top a thin layer of bread and butter, bake until tomatoes are throughout cooked.

*

Baked Squabs

To 6 fat squabs allow 1 pt. boiled chestnuts, remove shells, blanch and chop fine. Add good sized lump of butter and a few bread crumbs, a little salt and pepper to the nutmeats. Fill the birds with this dressing, pin a very thin strip of salt pork on breast of each. Place in roaster, salt, pepper and dredge with flour. Add 1 cup boiling water, bake ½ to 3/4 of an hour in good hot gravy. Boil and chop fine the giblets and add to the gravy. Garnish with parsley or water cress. Allow 1 bird for each guest.

*

Turkey Escallop

Make a pint of gravy from the bones and skin, chop the bits of meat picked from the bones very fine. Have ready a buttered pudding dish, with layer of dried or rolled bread or cracker crumbs; add a layer of minced turkey, and dot with bits of butter, seasoning with salt and pepper. Moisten each layer with some of the gravy, with milk and so continue until the dish is full. Let the top layer be of crumbs, seasoned and dotted with butter and moistened with gravy; or make a crust with crumbs wet with gravy and milk, mixed beaten up with two eggs. Spread it smoothly over the top about ¼ of an inch thick; invert a pie dish over it and bake in a moderate oven until it begins to bubble at the sides; remove the cover and brown.

*

Venison

Venison slices better if frozen. Slice extremely thin, roll in flour. Fry quickly in bacon fat and serve with crisp bacon. Must be well done. Venison is also delicious sliced thin and broiled and served with broiled bacon.

*

Roasted Partridges

Pluck the partridges, draw and truss them, and fasten some thin slices of fat bacon round them, roast for 15 minutes in a hot oven. Five minutes before dishing, take the bacon off, sprinkle a little salt over the birds and brown them. Put the partridges on a hot dish, and serve them with a sauceboatful of brown gravy.

*

❖❖❖

To fill holes in plaster — tear old newspapers into small bits, cover with water and cook until it forms a thin paste and apply with a small wooden paddle, pressing it in well. Let it harden twenty-four hours before you paper. This is as satisfactory as plastering, and has the additional advantage of being easily applied by a woman, if the men folks are busy. It is equally good for filling cracks in the floor or woodwork.

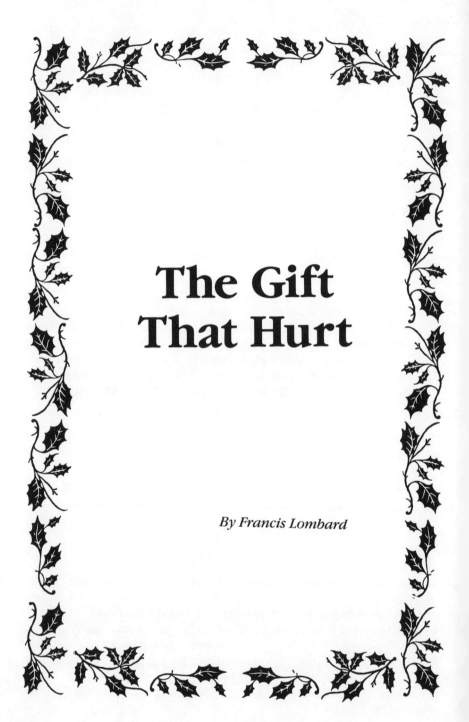

The Gift That Hurt

By Francis Lombard

This story took place during the Depression before the days of government welfare programs. Each community tried to help its own people as best it could. This is a true story of the attempts of the Wisconsin Land and Lumber Company in the small Upper Peninsula lumbering town of Hermansville and some of its salaried workers to do just that.

Angelena lifted the kitchen curtain and gazed out at the snowy road leading up the street. The sidewalk had long since been obliterated by the heavy snows of early winter and people just didn't bother to keep it shovelled. Dusk was falling and the last rays of the sun, low in the sky, gilded the broad expanse of the frozen mill pond with gold. Stumps of former giant trees stuck up through the snow at random and made long purple shadows. It was a scene that she loved, and gazing at this special time of day always had the power to lift her spirits.

She sighed because her spirits did not respond to the scene before her. She turned to the little kitchen and picked up a heavy stick of wood from the wood box and put it into the stove. As she lifted the lid to insert the wood, flames blazed up and their shadows brightened the darkening room. She did not turn on the lights. She pulled the coffee pot from the back of the stove toward the front where it would heat more quickly. She glanced at a basket of clothes she had been mending, some with patches on patches.

She looked at the supper table, set for six. Although the checkered cloth was gay and very clean, the table looked bare, for there was nothing else there, no relishes, no extras, nothing except the plates waiting to be filled. In the oven was a rabbit roasting with some potatoes.

Thank God, she thought, that her husband was a good shot or there would have been no rabbit. They didn't like rabbit that much and would have preferred a thick rich sauce with some raviolis with lots of good Italian cheese. She sighed. Good cheese cost money.

She shook herself. No use thinking about such things. They were lucky to be eating at all. This was in the middle of what everybody was calling THE DEPRESSION. She knew it was a troublesome time, although she could not understand why it had happened. She knew it was a bad time because so many strangers came by her house and those of her neighbors asking for a few potatoes or onions. Her husband said these men took the food down behind the depot in the woods and cooked it, everybody putting in what he had collected. Her husband called this place a HoBo Jungle. She didn't think the men were hobos. They looked too worried, too unhappy and desperate to be hobos. They said they were looking for work and she believed them, because many people in the little lumbering town were out of work too.

She didn't know what she and her family would have done if the owner of the lumber mill had not given each mill hand a few days of work at his job. They didn't earn much but it did help. Everyone was in the same boat. There was talk that if things didn't pick up soon, even this part time work would stop. She didn't know what she would do if this happened. She thought they could get by with the garden stuff they had raised last summer which she had canned or stored. Her husband could get a rabbit or a deer, providing the game warden turned his head. They still had to pay the rent and electricity. The children wore out their shoes and overalls. Life insurance had to be paid and their small contribution to St. Mary's Church on the hill. All these thoughts slipped through her head, but there was one subject she could not get up the courage to face.

Christmas was coming. What were they going to do about that? She pushed the thought from her mind and went again to the window to watch for her husband who was out cutting wood and the children who were at church for Catechism.

The sun had gone down and blue dusk had settled on the land. The little white company houses all in a row looked like identical ghosts lined up to swallow their people. Smoke from the chimneys went straight up, a sign of a cold windless night. The scene was as gloomy as her thoughts.

She spied her husband John, plodding up the road, his ax carried over his shoulder. Frosty breath streamed from his nostrils. His head was bent and weariness sat on his every movement.

"Poor man," she said softly. "He's discouraged, too, and tired. He's been out in the woods all day chopping wood to keep us warm."

Good that the wood was free! All the men had to do was cut it down and haul it home. She spared a kind thought for the owner of the mill who let his men cut the wood on his property. At least they could keep warm. Even if the wood was green, it would dry out and burn along with clippings of maple flooring from the factory. They lived in the kitchen to save wood, and the stiff little parlor with its lace curtains was icy cold. So were the beds to which they went at night, but at least they could keep each other warm. The children slept together but they didn't seem to mind the cold. Their long underwear, which they wore continuously and slept in for the week, seemed adequate.

She opened the door when she heard John on the porch, stamping the snow from his boots.

"Come in," she greeted. "Come in and get warm. Here, sit by the fire and I'll help you get your boots off."

He took off his heavy mackinaw and hung it on a peg on the back of the door along with his wool cloak. The leather covered mittens with their wool liners he slapped together to knock off the snow and then laid them on top of the wood box to dry. With a sigh he sank down on the chair beside the stove, a ripple of cold air coming off him as he did so. She felt it as she bent to unlace the boots, the ties stiff with clots of ice.

"We done a lot today," he said. "Antoine and I worked the crosscut saw and cut a lot of logs up into chunks. He thinks he can get a sleigh tomorrow and we can haul the wood home. He's a good worker, and we done more togehter than one man by hisself. We ought to be in pretty good shape for the winter if we can just get in a few days of cutting. At least we'll be warm and it won't cost nothing except the work."

She nodded. He went on.

"A man ought to work if he can find work. That's all a man wants is a chance to work and support his family. I don't mind hard work. Makes a man feel good to take care of his wife and family. I don't understand what's happening to this country. I don't know how this Depression works. First, everybody's working — and then everything stops. Antoine and me were talking about it today. He doesn't understand either."

He stood up and stretched his aching muscles. She poured him a cup of coffee. When he had taken a sip she said, "The children will be home soon, and we got a good supper. I fixed that rabbit you got. It's in the over right now."

He looked at the bank calendar hanging over the wood box. It said the month was December, the year 1933. December twenty-five had been printed in red to draw attention to this special day. This was a very special day. It was the birthday of Jesus. He knew they always celebrated it joyfully. Angelena saw him looking at the calendar. She looked at him when he turned to her. There was a question in their eyes.

*

On another street was a large spacious house, built back from the road, surrounded by huge elms. It was the home of the company's owner. In the living room his wife Anne was handing out cups of coffee to a small group of women gathered about the blazing fireplace. She was a pretty woman in her forties whose face revealed great kindness. Her manner was unassuming as she talked to her friends. Some listened in surprise; a few nodded in agreement; other questioned with their eyes.

"I have asked you all to come here today for a very special reason - not that there has to be a special reason for you to come here." She laughed. "You know that."

The women smiled and drank their coffee and nibbled on the cookies being passed.

"Harold has a project in mind, and he thought that you would be just the people to help him. As you know times are very bad. The Depression is deepening. There just is no business. He has tried to keep the mills going and the factory running on a limited basis. He has portioned out the work among the men so that each will have a little time in and get some wages. He knows each man and how hard it is for them to get along right now."

The women looked sober and worried. They knew very well what she was talking about. Their husbands had been kept on, although at reduced salaries. Their husbands were the heads of departments or worked in the office. They were the bare backbones of the organization. They didn't know how long the organization could be kept together if no business came in. The women also thought of the five percent taken from their husbands' salaries to be put into a fund to help other workers not so fortunate.

"As you know, Christmas is coming. Some of us are wondering how the families will fare, especially the children who do not realize what is happening," she continued.

"I've been wondering about that too," said one of the women. "Our own Christmas will be cut down, but we'll have something. I hate to see children disappointed at Christmas. They are so little."

"You've got to the heart of the matter," said Anne. "That is what Harold has asked me to do something about — with your help of course."

"Of course, of course!" they all chorused. "What should we do?"

"He wondered if we could fix up some baskets and have them delivered without anyone knowing where they came from. We could use the money from the fund collected from the salaries." And she smiled.

"I like the idea of it being done secretly," spoke up one woman.

"I do too," said another. "Then their feelings won't be hurt. Some of them are really proud."

Another woman spoke up. "I live near a family and know what they need and the ages and sizes of their children. Perhaps we could work it that way."

The women, busily planning, putting names down on paper, smiling and talking, went to work with great enthusiasm.

A few days before Christmas a sleigh loaded with bulging baskets was driven around the town. The driver delivered his load from a list he had in his pocket. He went to each door and knocked. "Merry Christmas," he said, handing in a basket.

At some of the houses people who answered his knock were too astonished to say anything except stammer a thanks and receive the basket. At other doors, people took the basket, but they did not smile or say thank you.

Angelena had been watching through the kitchen curtains the driver's progress up the street. She saw him carry baskets to the different doors. She saw the doors open and the baskets taken inside. Then she saw the driver stop at her door and come up the walk. She dropped the curtain and listend to the knocking. Her heart pounded and she held her breath. She did not answer the door. The knocking grew more insistent, but still she did not answer. Finally the sound of footsteps faded away. She looked through the curtain and saw the driver getting back into his sleigh. The basket was standing all alone on the porch. All day it sat there and Angelena struggled with herself.

At dusk she went again to her favorite scene, the mill pond at sunset. When the sun had faded and all was grey, she opened the door and took in the basket. She wept as she did so.

The Home Messenger Book of Tested Receipts, 1878

Dedicated to the patrons and friends of the Detroit Home of the Friendless

Good New England Coffee

For a family of six, take six large tablespoonfuls of best Java coffee well browned and ground (not too fine), beat into it half an egg and one cup of cold water. After it is thoroughly beaten, let it stand half an hour, well covered. Then put into coffee pot, pour on two and a half quarts of boiling water and put on the stove, stir once or twice at first, to prevent burning. Let it scald fifteen or twenty minutes. If desired to be very nice, beat up eight instead of six tablespoonfuls coffee; put six in the pot to boil twenty minutes, and about five minutes before it is done, throw in the rest and cover quickly.

*

Baking Powder Biscuits

Sift 1 quart of flour, 2 teaspoons of Calumet baking powder, 1 teaspoon of salt into a bowl. Add sufficient milk to make a soft dough. Knead lightly. Roll out about one-half inch thick. Cut with small cutter and place a little apart on baking tin. Bake in quick oven for twenty minutes.

*

Celery Cheese

Take a head or two of celery, wash thoroughly and boil until tender. Drain well and cut into small pieces. Have ready 1/2 pint of creamy and rich drawn butter, add pepper, salt and on ounce or two of grated cheese to it. Put the celery into the sauce for a few minutes, then fill buttered scallop shells with the mixture. Scatter grated cheese over the top and bake five or ten minutes in a quick oven, when the cheese should be evenly browned.

*

Mushrooms and Bacon

Take a few slices of bacon and fry them in the usual manner; when nearly done, add a dozen mushrooms and fry them slowly until they are cooked; add a little pepper and salt; serve hot for breakfast.

*

Welsh Rarebit

Cut ½ pound of cheese very fine. Wet chafing dish with ale. Put in a piece of butter the size of hickory nut. Place dish over flame, heat butter to boiling, then put cheese in slowly, alternating with a little ale until all cheese is melted. Add 1 teaspoon of mustard, a dash of cayenne pepper, and salt to taste. Lift with spoon and cook until it will not string. Serve on toast or crackers.

*

Fruit Cake

1 lb. raisins, 1 lb. currants, ½ lb. citron, 1 pint hickory nut meats, 1 grated nutmeg, 3½ cups of flour, teaspoons of baking powder, 1 cup of molasses, 2 cups of brown sugar, 3 eggs, 1 cup of butter, 1 cup of milk; steam 4 hours. Put on top grate and brown top of cake when done.

Fruit Salad

Fruit salads, as they are called, are very popular, and often served for a first course. Have dainty, pretty glasses and fill them with chopped pineapple, thinly sliced bananas, white grapes cut in halves and seeded, the pulp and juice of an orange, and candied cherries. Cover with a dressing made of 4 tablespoonsful of powered sugar, 1 gill of sherry, 1 tablespoon of maraschino juice, and 2 of champagne. Stir until the sugar is dissolved and then pour over the fruit and let them stand in a cool place an hour before service.

*

Chicken Salad

Cook chicken and shred very fine. For dressing, use 1 egg well beaten, 1 teaspoon of melted butter, 1 teaspoon of mustard, 1 tablespoon of sugar, a little salt, 1/2 cup of vinegar, 1 cup of sweet cream, and chopped celery. Mix egg, mustard, butter, sugar, salt and vinegar. Boil until it thickens. Cool and add cream. Stir in shredded meat.

*

Cream and Milk for Coffee

Sweet, rich cream, well beaten to free from lumps, is best for coffee, but boiling fresh milk is a good substitute. The white of an egg, thoroughly beaten and added to thin cream or rich milk, is also very nice.

*

Tea and Coffee for Children

Tea and coffee for children is as bad in its effects as its use is universal. Dr. Ferguson found that children so fed only grew four pounds per annum between the ages of thirteen and sixteen; while those who got milk night and morning grew fifteen pounds each year. This needs no commentary. The deteriorated physique of tea and coffee fed children, as seen in their lessened power to resist disease, is notorious among the medical men of factory districts.

*

The Alma Cook Book

Ladies of the First Presbyterian Church, 1899

Cream Puffs

Boil one half-pint of water. When boiling, stir in two-thirds of a cup of butter, one and one-thirds cups of flour. Let it cook carefully. Take from the fire. Let it stand till cool. Beat in carefully, one at a time, five eggs. Drop on buttered tins. Bake 35 minutes in moderate oven.

*

Cream for Inside

Boil one pint of milk. While boiling, stir a little of mixture into two beaten eggs. Add eggs to milk with 1 cup of sugar and 1 cup of flour. When nearly cool, stir in butter ¹/₂ the size of an egg and flavor with Jennings' extract of vanilla. When the cakes are warm, split at the sides and fill.

*

Yorkshire Pudding

A very good accompaniment to a roast beef.

One pint of milk, four eggs (whites and yolks beaten separately), one teaspoon of salt, and two teaspoons of baking powder. Mix well and add in two cups of sifted flour. It should be mixed very smooth, about the consistency of cream. Take two common biscuit tins, dip some of the drippings from the meat into these pans, pour half the pudding in each pan, set in hot oven, bake quickly and serve as soon as done.

*

Swiss Eggs

6 eggs, 1/4 pound cheese, 1/3 cupful of cream or milk, 2 tablespoons of butter, 1 teaspoon of mustard, 1/2 teaspoon of salt, one-tenth of a teaspoonful of cayenne. Cut the cheese into thin shavings, butter an egg dish or small china platter and spread the cheese in it. Upon the cheese, distribute in small portions the remainder of the butter. Mix salt, cayenne, mustard and cream. Pour half the mixture over the cheese, break the eggs into the dish and after pouring over them the remaining liquid, place in the oven. Bake eight minutes.

*

A Cook's Tour: Choice Recipes

Michigan State Federation of Women's Clubs, 1934

Nut Fingers

$^{1}/_{2}$ pound butter
3 level cups sifted flour
3 heaping tbsp. sugar
1 cup cut-up pecans
Vanilla and pinch of salt
Cream butter and sugar well, add flour, then pecans. When adding last cup of flour it is best to use hands. Roll on palms of hands enough dough to make a roll the size of large finger. Put in refrigerator, overnight or longer, until ready to bake. Bake in flat or low pan in moderate oven. Watch closely. When light brown, remove from oven. When still warm (not hot), sprinkle with confectioners sugar. This makes 45 or 50 fingers.

*

English Christmas Pudding

1 lb. beef suet
1 1/2 lb. stoned raisins
1 lb. sultana raisins
1/2 lb. currants
1/2 lb. mixed fruit peel
1 grated nutmeg
1 oz. ground cinnamon
1 oz. mixed spice
4 oz. flour
1 lb. bread crumbs
1/4 lb. almonds
8 eggs
The juice and rind of 2 lemons
2 wine glasses brandy
1/2 pint of milk
Pinch of salt

Skin and chop the suet finely, clean the fruit, shred finely the mixed peel, grate the lemon rind. Put the dry ingredients in a bowl and mix together. Add the milk, stir in the eggs one at a time, add the brandy and strained lemon juice. Mix thoroughly until well blended together. Put the mixture into well buttered pudding bowls and steam 8 hours.

*

Sauce for Christmas Pudding

1/2 lb. butter
1 lb. confectioners sugar
1/4 cup cream
Enough brandy to taste

Cream the butter, add the sugar and beat together, then add the cream and brandy. Sprinkle with grated nutmeg.

*

Sweet Potato Pie

2 cups mashed sweet potatoes
2 cups sugar
1 cup butter
1 cup sweet milk
6 eggs
Flavor to taste with nutmeg, lemon or cinnamon

Boil, mash and strain potatoes through sieve, measure, add butter and milk. Beat yolks of eggs with sugar; add potatoes. Beat whites of eggs stiff and add last.

Pour into a pie crust and bake thirty minutes in moderate oven or until done. If gas oven is used, bake near the bottom of oven in order to cook at bottom. Brush over the pastry with cooking oil or melted shortening before putting in the mixture. This makes two large pies.

*

Wally Bronner at the CHRISTmas Wonderland in Franken-muth.

Wally Bronner: Michigan's Mr. Christmas

By Nancy Marcetti

"Dear Santa,

"I struggled with myself this year over how much emphasis to place on you versus giving the real meaning of Christ's birth at this time to my four children (1 1/2 to 7 years)."

Many parents face the dilemma of explaining Christmas to their children. How should they celebrate the holiday? With presents or prayer? Santa or Savior? There was a time when Christmas meant gathering together to celebrate the birth of Christ. Those days, for the most part, have given way to gifts, cookies and department stores.

Christmas has become a commercial holiday, and many children grow up without knowing the true meaning of Christmas.

For those children and their parents, a glimmer of hope does exist.

"We came to see you though, and I want you to know that the love of Jesus I saw in your eyes made you and Christmas go together beautifully. Your whole presence radiated God's love."

This letter was written to a man who is in the very thick of Christmas commercialism — a man who attempts to mix true Christmas spirit among the glitz and glitter.

This glimmer of hope was first recognized when a 12-year-old boy, Wallace Bronner of Frankenmuth, entered a watercolor in a local contest sponsored by Zehnder's restaurant. Little did he know his creativity would someday put him at the zenith of the Christmas display business.

Without realizing his true calling in life, Wally, 16, showed an interest in chemical engineering and thought of attending Michigan State University.

"It wasn't that I was particularly fond of engineering, but because it was the 'in' thing to do," Wally recalled.

A friend and local church and community leader, Dr. Clem Kirchgeorg, believed Wally should become a writer because he was creative. Kirchgeorg didn't push the idea, but instead advised him to find a job he could do 24 hours a day without tiring of it.

Wally followed the advice quite by accident. He was decorating the windows of his Aunt Hattie's grocery store when two businessmen from Clare approached him. They were impressed with Wally's window dressing abilities and hired him to paint lamppost signs for their city. From there, other cities in neighboring areas began placing orders, forcing Wally to hire part-time help to keep up with the demand.

He never made it to MSU because he became absorbed in what was to become the largest year-round display of Christmas items.

Business increased, and Wally expanded his inventory. Still, Wally had no idea he would sell more than lamppost signs, street garlands and exterior building decorations until 1960.

"Later, someone asked if we sold department store decorations, which we didn't, until the request was made. Another inquiry was made about home decorations, and they were also added," Wally explained.

This continued until Bronner's entered all facets of the Christmas industry. Once fully immersed in Christmas, the stores in downtown Frankenmuth displaying Bronner's items became so crowded doormen were hired to control the overflow. Lines of people waiting to enter created traffic jams. The little enterprise on Tuscola Street was about to enter the world of big business.

The jump to big business came when Wally and Irene, his wife, realized they needed more space to accommodate the crowd and their ever-increasing inventory. The result was Bronner's CHRISTmas Wonderland.

The new store is located at 25 Christmas Lane in Frankenmuth. The town, founded by German Lutheran missionaries in 1845, has long attracted tourists with its old world hospitality, quaint atmosphere and famous chicken dinners at the Bavarian Inn and Zehnder's. However, Frankenmuth can attribute much of its current success to Wally. Each year more than three million people visit the town of 4,500 residents.

Bronner's is open all year except for Thanksgiving, Christmas, New Year's Day, and Easter.

"I believe people come throughout the year to experience the

Christmas magic and prepare for their next Christmas, be it 90-degrees or 90-below," Wally stated.

Visitors can see and feel the Christmas spirit by wandering around the fully carpeted showrooms, which cover one-and-a-half acres (one-and-a-third football fields). The first thing you notice is the soft, continuous flow of Christmas carols echoing as you walk through the aisles of color, lights and action. The cheerful sales-women wear German dresses, called dirndls, and the salesmen wear red vests and Christmasy ties. Normally Bronner's employs about 185 people, but that number escalates during the last part of the year.

"We need about 350 employees during our peak season, which runs July through December," Wally confirmed.

Throughout the spacious showroom are large decorations. One-third of the salesroom is devoted to the Tannenbaum area, which displays 260 decorated trees, over 6,000 stules of glass ornaments and a wide variety of lights. All the trees are decorated in themes: a towering pine stands covered with large red bows, poinsettia flowers, lights and garlands; dwarfed by this tree is the toddler's tree adorned with colorful crush-proof ornaments and lights; across the room is a patriotic tree decorated with Lady Liberty and red, white and blue lights.

Bronner's program center displays select ornaments from distant countries such as mouth-blown glass ornaments from Austria and Poland. Also displayed here are Bronner's original, custom-designed ornaments.

The center houses the store's complete collection of Hummels. Eighteen-minute slide presentations of Bronner's history are run throughout the day.

Bronner's goal is to provide people with every decoration they could possibly want to express their individual feelings of Christmas. In order to fulfill that goal, Bronner's stocks more than 50,000 items, which fall into one of three categories: religious, traditional, and toyland.

To ensure every visitor will find something to suit his or her taste, Bronner's imports items from places such as Uruguay and Sri Lanka. Wally's favorite part of the business is finding additional, unique items and then observing people as they react to the wide varieties of merchandise. The store carries cornshuck and clay nativity scenes from Czechoslovakia and Peru, and has Bibles in 33 languages. Every continent is represented in some way at Bronner's, and Wally likes working with people from all of them. He did say some countries are more helpful than others.

"The ones that celebrate Christmas religiously are the most helpful because they fit in with the idea we are promoting," Wally said.

The lack of religious symbolism Wally saw when first starting out prompted him to create his own ornaments. His first one was a clear bulb with Mary, Joseph and Jesus inside. He has never had a difficult time coming up with ideas. Sometimes it is just a matter of taking an old design and presenting it in a new way.

"Christmas is the observance of Christ's birthday; we want to have decorations so people can express this in their own way," Wally said.

But isn't this commercialism? Isn't Wally Bronner making a living off Christmas? Wally has been asked these questions many times.

"It isn't wrong if it's done in a Lord-pleasing way," he stated.

The commercialism of Christmas gives Christians the opportunity to witness what Christmas is all about. If Christians don't celebrate, who will, Wally asked.

The most important thing Wally has learned is not how to capitalize on Christmas or create an ornament, but something much more valuable.

"Trust in the Lord. Put faith in Him and try to follow His commands," Wally said.

It is this trust that contributes to the unique appearance and presentation of Bronner's; winning the Golden Santa award in 1986 is proof of that. This award was designed to advance the industry in its creative approach to Christmas. It is given by a group of ornament suppliers to the establishment that shows worldwide creativity and new ideas for the setup and presentation of Christmas articles. Bronner's was picked from a list of twelve finalists, beating out the prestigious Harrod's of London. It was a complete surprise to the family.

"We wondered if we were worthy of it," Wally said. Now the award rests as an incentive to make sure Bronner's will always deserve the praise it received.

Winning the Golden Santa award was not an individual effort. Wally has a staff of talented, dedicated and loyal employees, of which he is very proud. It isn't hard to be loyal to Wally. You don't have to work with him for years to discover how sincere and thoughtful he is. He is always willing to talk with visitors, and treats everyone the same, as if he or she were a star. Many pictures of famous people hang in Bronner's showroom, but Wally is not impressed.

"To me, everyone is a celebrity," he said.

However, there is one person who sticks in Wally's mind—Dr. Ken Taylor, who wrote the Contemporary Bible. Wally believes it is quite an accomplishment to be the author of a Bible. Taylor presented Bronner's with his ten millionth copy.

Meeting people like Taylor keeps Wally's job interesting; variation is the key. Besides being at the showroom most of the time, Wally speaks at many engagements and socializes with people at various functions. He feels it is a special blessing he has not grown tired of the business. He said it helps to believe in what you are doing. After all these years, he never once wished he went into another line of work.

"It seems like I've been with my hobby lifelong," he said.

His real hobbies are few. He enjoys taking photos, relishing the scenery on trips, and being with his family. Even on vacation, Wally finds it hard to turn off the business.

"If I could, I'd build a desk and chair out of sand and then wait for the phone to ring," he joked.

When he is absent, the business is in the capable hands of his son, Wayne; daughters, Carla and Maria; daughter-in-law, Lorene; son-in-law, Bob; and wife, Irene. However, "Mr. Christmas" has no immediate plans to leave the company. Instead, he will continue spreading the joy of Christmas to people of all ages in his unique way.

Anyone who visits Bronner's CHRISTmas Wonderland and meets Wally can see he is the living example of Bronner's theme: Enjoy CHRISTmas! It is His birthday! Enjoy life! It is His way!

What better way to introduce children to the true meaning of Christmas than to meet "Mr. Christmas" himself?

Choice Recipes

Methodist Epsicopal Ladies Aid Society of Grand Ledge

Plum Pudding

A plum pudding that is not over rich wants a cupful of chopped suet, a cupful of sour milk, a cupful of molasses, a cupful each of raisins and figs, minced fine, three cupfuls and a half of flour, two eggs, a teaspoonful of cloves, two teaspoonfuls of cinnamon, a grated nutmeg, a little salt and a teaspoonful of soda dissolved in a little warm water. Fill a mold two-thirds full with the mixture and steam three hours.

*

Lady Fingers

Four egg yolks beaten thick, two-thirds cup flour sifted twice, dash of salt. Beat thoroughly, six egg whites beaten stiff, add two-thirds cup powdered sugar, fold into the first mixture. Bake in lady finger tins twenty minutes and just before putting in slow oven sprinkle with powdered sugar.

*

Christmas at Meadowbrook Hall in Rochester.

Chocolate Cookies

One-half cup powdered sugar, four squares chocolate grated, one-half teaspoon vanilla. Mix and fold in three egg whites beaten very stiff, drop on waxed paper from teaspoon and bake in slow oven.

*

Snow Flakes

Use your three egg yolks left from chocolate cookies, beaten with one-quarter teaspoon salt, one-half teaspoon cinnamon, flour — enough to roll very thin. Cut in long narrow strips and fry in very hot fat. When done dust with powdered sugar.

*

Fruit Cookies

Cream one-half a cup of butter with one cup of sugar, beat two eggs very light and add them, then stir in four tablespoonfuls of sour milk into which has been beaten one-half a teaspoonful of baking soda. Mix together a cup of chopped raisins and one of chopped nuts, flour them and stir them into the batter with one-half teaspoonful of ground cloves and one teaspoonful of ground cinnamon. Fold in quickly two cups of flour and drop the mixture by spoonfuls on greased paper. Bake in a moderate oven.

*

Soft Maple Caramels

One cup maple syrup, one-half cup cream, lump butter. Boil until it will form a soft ball when dropped in cold water. Let stand until cool, then beat to a cream. Put in buttered tins and cut in squares.

*

Always sit down to wash the dishes. Have trays for the dishes bound for different places, and place them on the proper trays when wiped. (Use tray in the same way when clearing the table.) Wipe all grease off of dishes with bits of paper or old cloth. Try a dishcloth of quilted mosquito netting. Remember, "it takes a lady to wash dishes."

Pie Crust

To make good pie crusts, the dough must be handled as little as possible. There is a rule of one, two, three, which, if followed, will insure nice crispy crusts. One pint sifted flour, two tablespoons lard, three tablespoons water and a pinch of salt. This amount is sufficient for one pie with top crust.

*

Rhubarb and Raisin Pie

Chop fine one pound of rhubarb and one and one-half cupfuls of seeded raisins. Add one pint of sugar and two well beaten eggs. This will make two pies; make with top and bottom crusts.

*

A Novel Cranberry Pie

Take a good sized cupful of cranberries, cut them in two and put them in cold water to draw out the seeds. Mix a tablespoonful of flour with a cupful of sugar, and then add slowly a scant cupful of boiling water and a half cupful of raisins stoned and cut in two. Lift the cranberries out of the cold water, which should be thrown away, and mix them with the other ingredients. Bake between two crusts. Sometimes a teaspoonful of vanilla is added.

*

Brown Bread

Mix two cups of sweet milk with one cup of sour, add two cups of white meal, one cup of flour, one cup of molasses, two teaspoonfuls of baking soda and a little salt. Mix well, turn into a mold, and steam for three hours, then set in the oven for five minutes before turning out.

*

Peaches in Turkish Mode

Peaches cooked in Turkish fashion are served with boiled rice. Peel the peaches by plunging them in boiling water, then remove the stone through slit in one side, without injuring the shape of the peach. Fill hollows with seeded raisins and arrange in baking dish; sprinkle liberally with sugar and set in hot oven twenty minutes. Have ready a dish lined with boiled rice. Spread over it peaches, and serve with dressing made of cocoanut milk thickened with corn starch and sweetened with granulated sugar.

*

Maraschino Cherries

Weigh the stemmed cherries, after removing the stones. To every two pounds of fruit make a syrup of a pound of sugar and a half-gill of water. Heat to boiling, stirring to prevent burning, and pour over the cherries while warm, but not hot. Stand for an hour, then put over the fire and heat very slowly. Boil for just five minutes, take out the cherries with a skimmer, and lay on platters, allowing the syrup to boil for twenty minutes more. To every five pounds of fruit allow a pint of maraschino, and add this to the syrup just before taking from the fire. Put the cherries in jars, fill to overflowing with the maraschino syrup and seal.

*

Fruit Salad

Peel two large oranges and cut each lobe into three pieces. Remove the seeds from a cup of Malaga grapes; shell and break into bits a dozen English walnut meats. Mix these ingredients and set on the ice until very cold. Line a chilled bowl with crisp lettuce leaves, put the fruit in the center of the bowl and cover well with mayonnaise or French dressing.

*

Waldorf Salad

One cup sour apples cut in thin slices, one cup celery cut in small pieces. Add one tablespoon lemon juice, one-half cup walnut meats. Season with salt and pepper and mix with mayonnaise.

*

Shrimp And Tomato Salad

Put boiled shrimps on ice until very cold. Strip the skins from the large ripe tomatoes and scoop out the insides. Set these also in the ice to get chilled. Fill the hollowed tomatoes with the shrimps, set each tomato on a leaf of lettuce and pour mayonnaise dressing over all.

*

Currantade

Crush one quart of currants and one cup of raspberries, add two and a half quarts of water and strain or squeeze the juice from a jelly bag; add the juice of one lemon and sweeten to taste; close tightly in jars and set on ice till ready to use. It is better to let stand several hours to get very cold and the sugar well dissolved. A few whole berries may be added just before serving.

*

Strawberryade

Mash one pint of strawberries, add the juice of four lemons and five pints of water. Strain and add about two cups of water. It is best to sweeten to taste, as some lemons are more sour than others. When serving put a few nice whole berries in each glass.

*

Envelopes for drinking cups — It seems almost unnecessary to caution people against drinking from public cups on trains and boats, yet this is a common practice, even in states where travelers flock because of tuberculosis. Always carry with you a few new envelopes and cut these in two diagonally, making triangular drinking cups which can be used once and thrown away.

Cheese Mold

Beat the yolks of three eggs. Mix in a quarter of a teaspoon each of salt, pepper and mustard, and pour on slowly one cup of hot milk. Return to the fire and cook like custard; add one teaspoon of gelatine, which has been soaked in four tablespoons of cold water, strain over one-half cup of grated cheese, stir over hot water until the mixture begins to thicken, fold in one cup of cream beaten stiff, turn into a mold to become firm. When ready to serve cut into slices and serve on brown or graham bread.

*

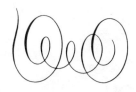

Cheese Balls

The white of two eggs, two ounces of grated cheese, salt and cayenne. Beat the eggs to a stiff broth, stir in the cheese, salt and cayenne pepper. Shape the mixture into balls the size of marbles and drop them into boiling lard. Fry them for about five minutes, till a golden brown, drain well and serve with grated cheese.

*

Cheese Fondu

Grease a baking dish and put in one cupful of grated cheese, one cupful of bread crumbs, one-half a teaspoon of salt, a quarter of a teaspoon of pepper, a small pinch of dried mustard and a dash of cayenne pepper. Mix all together. Beat an egg, then add one cup of milk and pour this over the baking dish. Melt a large lump of butter and pour over the top. Put in a hot oven and bake from 15 to 20 minutes, being careful it does not burn.

*

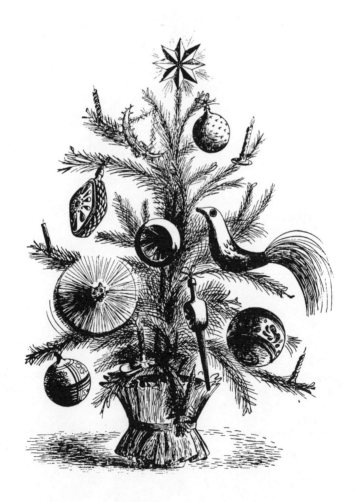

Reminiscences Of Early Days On Mackinac Island

(An account of Christmas festivities during the early 1800s on Mackinac Island)

From the diary of Elizabeth Therese Baird

The Catholic faith prevailing, it followed as a matter of course that the special holidays of the church were always observed in a memorable, pleasant manner in one's own family, in which some friends and neighbors would participate. Some weeks before Christmas, the denizens of the island met in turn at each other's homes, and read the prayers, chanted psalms, and unfailingly repeated the litany of the saints.

On Christmas eve, both sexes would read and sing, the service lasting till midnight. After this, a reveillon (midnight treat) would be partaken of by all. The last meeting of this sort which I attended, was at our own home, in 1823. This affair was considered the high feast of the season, and no pains were spared to make the accompanying meal as good as the island afforded. The cooking was done at on open fire. I wish I could remember in full the bill of fare: however, I will give all that I recall. We will begin with the roast pig; roast goose; chicken pie; round of beef, a la mode; pattes d'ours (bear's paws, called so from the shape, and made of chopped meat in crust, corresponding to rissoles); sausage; head-cheese; soups; small fruit preserves; small cakes. Such was the array. No one was expected to partake of every dish, unless he chose.

Christmas was observed as a holy day. The children were kept at home, and from play, until nearly night-time, when they would be allowed to run out and bid their friends a "Merry Christmas," spending the evening, however, at home with the family, the service of prayer and song being observed as before mentioned. All would sing; there was no particular master — it was the sentiment that was so pleasing to us; the music we did not care so much for.

As soon as la fete de Noel, or Christmas-tide, had passed, all the young people were set at work to prepare for New Year's. On the eve of that day, great preparations were made by a certain class of elderly men, usually fishermen, who went from house to house in grotesque dress, singing and dancing. Following this, they would receive gifts. Their song was often quite terrifying to little girls, as the gift asked for in the song was la fille ainee, the eldest daughter. The song ran thus:

Bon jour, le Maitre et al Maitresse,
Et tout le monde du longer.
Si vous voulez nous rien donner, dites-le nous:
Nous vous demandons seulement la fille ainee!

As they were always expected, everyone was prepared to receive them. This ended the last day of the year. After evening prayer in the family, the children would retire early. At the dawn of the New Year, each child would go to the bedside of its parents to receive their benediction — a most beautiful custom. My sympathies always went out to children who had no parents near.

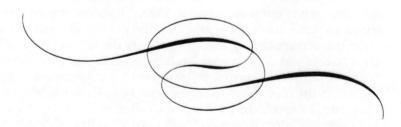

Tried and True, Recipes and Suggestions

*Ladies of the Presbyterian Methodist Episcopal Church —
Detroit, 1901*

Orange Salad

Get large, good-shaped oranges, cut them in two, crosswise, and take out the pulp, bruising as little as possible; cut the pulp into small, nicely shaped pieces and have mixed nuts, walnuts, peanuts and almonds, chopped. Pour the dressing over the nuts and fill each half orange shell with a mixture of chopped nuts and oranges and pour some more dressing on top. Set each half on a crisp lettuce leaf.

Dressing: One-half cup of vinegar, one-half teaspoonful mustard, one-half teaspoonful salt, one big teaspoonful sugar, one teaspoonful cornstarch, yolks of two eggs, one teaspoonful butter, one-half cup of cream. Put vinegar on to heat and mix mustard in a little cold vinegar and add; then add the salt, sugar and butter and yolks of eggs beaten and thinned with a little milk; dissolve cornstarch in a little milk, stir until it thickens, then take from the fire and add cream slowly, stirring all the time to prevent curdling. Add more cream if too thick.

*

A Nice Cornstarch Pudding

One pint sweet milk, three tablespoons cornstarch, salt, one-half cup sugar; cook in double boiler until thick; add the beaten whites of three eggs. Put into cups with strawberries, cherries, or any kind of fruit in the bottom; when cold turn out and serve with custard made of the yolks of the eggs and milk sweetened, and cook until like cream. To be eaten cold.

*

Cherry Dessert

Take the juice from a can of cherries, add one cup water, one cup sugar, one teaspoon butter; put into a saucepan and when it comes to a boil drop in dumplings made by taking one cup flour, one teaspoon baking powder, one-half cup milk, a pinch of salt. (This will make enough for six persons.) Keep closely covered and boil ten minutes. Serve with the liquid in which they have been cooked, for sauce. This is a nice dessert, easily made, and can be varied by using strawberries and raspberries, instead of cherries, when a smaller quantity of sugar should be used.

*

Fruit Pudding

One cup sour milk, two cups bread crumbs, one cup flour, one-half cup butter, one cup chopped raisins (seeded), two eggs, one cup sugar, one teaspoon soda, spice to taste. Steam two hours.

Sauce: One-half cup butter, one cup pulverized sugar, the white of one egg, beaten, two tablespoons sweet cream, nutmeg. Do not tire beating this, as the longer it is beaten the nicer it is.

*

Apple Pudding

Two cups bread crumbs, one-fourth cup butter, two cups sliced apples, one-half cup sugar, grated rind and juice of one lemon, a little nutmeg. Put a layer of bread crumbs in the bottom of a pudding dish, then a layer of the apples and sprinkle with the sugar, nutmeg and lemon; then another layer of crumbs and apples. Bake until apples are tender, covering the first half hour. Serve hot with whipped cream.

*

Strawberry Sherbet

One quart of berries mashed; sprinkle over these one pint of sugar, add the juice of one lemon, and a half-pint of water in which has been dissolved a tablespoonful of gelatine. Freeze as you would ice cream.

*

Whipped Cream

Take a pint of good, thick, sweet cream, very cold; put it in a large platter, and beat it up as stiff as the whites of eggs; sweeten with one-half cup of sugar and flavor with lemon or vanilla. Put it in a fruit dish and dot it over with jelly. If the cream is warm it will not whip, and if it is frozen after it is whipped it is all the better.

*

Cranberry Sauce

After removing all soft berries, put them in a granite pan with a little water; stew until all are broken, strain through colander to remove indigestible skins; return to fire and boil. Take from fire and sweeten.

*

Fig Jelly

Soak one rounding tablespoon gelatine in one-quarter cup of coffee; when soft add three-quarters cup boiling coffee, one cup light brown sugar, one-half cup figs, chopped fine; pour in a mould and serve with whipped cream.

*

Snow

Put one large cup of hot water in a double boiler; stir in two tablespoons cornstarch dissolved in cold water, add the whites of two eggs well beaten. Cook ten minutes, stirring often. Turn out in moulds.

Sauce: Two-thirds cup sugar, yolks of two eggs, piece of butter size of walnut, one cup of milk; beat all together and cook in double boiler. Flavor to taste. Serve cold.

*

Strawberry Sauce

One large tablespoon butter beaten to a cream. Add gradually one and one-half cups powdered sugar, and the beaten white of one egg. Beat till very light, and just before serving add one pint mashed strawberries.

*

Sauce For Plum or Suet Pudding

To make a bowlful, take a piece of butter size of an egg and beat it with one cup powdered sugar until it is a light cream; put one coffee cup water in a small tin saucepan and add one large teaspoon flour rubbed in a little cold water; cook till it is like a thin starch; pour it slowly into the creamed butter. If the beating be not stopped, the whole sauce will rise and be foamy as sea-froth; flavor to liking.

*

Mountain Dew

To one pint of sweet milk, add one-half cup rolled crackers, four tablespoons dessicated cocoanut, one-quarter cup of sugar and the well beaten yolks of two eggs, and one-half teaspoon lemon extract. Bake from twenty to thirty minutes. Beat the whites of eggs very stiff, add one-half cup of sugar, spread on top and set in the oven to brown.

*

Installing Christmas decorations near the Capitol in Lansing.

Orange Marmalade

One peck apples, one dozen oranges, four lemons. Boil apples until tender and put in a bag to drain, saving juice. Peel oranges very thin; boil the thin bits of skin two hours, and throw away the water. Mix juice of apples, the juice and soft pulp of oranges and lemons, boil twenty minutes. Add an equal amount of sugar and boil until it jellies. Just before putting into tumblers, add the orange peel.

*

Cucumber Salad

Four dozen medium-sized cucumbers, eighteen small onions peeled and chopped very fine; sprinkle over them three-fourths pint fine table salt, put in sieve and drain overnight. In the morning, add one teacup mustard seed, one-half cup whole black pepper; mix well and cover with cider vinegar.

*

Apple Tea

Two finely flavored pippins, one quart of cold water, as much ginger as will lie on a silver dime, sugar to taste. Pare and slice the apples, leaving the seeds in. Pack with the ginger in a glass or stone jar, pour in the water, put on the top loosely, and set in a kettle of cold water. Let it boil until the apple is broken to pieces. Strain while hot, squeezing hard. Strain again through flannel without pressing and let it get cold. Sweeten and ice.

*

Pineapple Lemonade

One pint water, one cup sugar, one quart ice water, one can grated pineapple, juice of three lemons. Make a syrup by boiling sugar and water ten minutes. Add the pineapple and lemon juice. Cool and strain and add the ice water. Tea, oranges, strawberries, cherries and other fruits may be added.

*

Unfermented Grape Juice

Sort grapes and place in porcelain kettle with just enough water to cover; boil until skins burst; strain, add half as much sugar as juice. Boil ten minutes. Seal and keep in a cool, dark place.

*

Raspberry Vinegar

To four quarts of red raspberries, put enough vinegar to cover, and let them stand twenty-four hours; scale and strain it; add one pound of sugar to one pint of juice; boil it twenty minutes and bottle. It is then ready for use and will keep for years. To one glass of water, add a great spoonful. It is very nice.

*

Raspberry Shrub

Place red raspberries in stone jar; cover with good cider vinegar, let stand overnight; next morning strain; to one pint of juice add one pint of sugar. Boil ten minutes. Bottle while hot.

*

Elderberry Shrub

Three quarts of fruit, mashed, one quart vinegar; let stand over night; strain through two cloths; add one measure of sugar to two of fruit. Boil ten minutes.

*

Potatoes on the Half Shell

Take six good-sized, smooth potatoes. Bake about one hour. When done, cut in two lengthways and with a spoon carefully scoop out the potato into a hot bowl. Mash fine and add two rounding tablespoonfuls of butter, about half a cup of hot milk, a rounding teaspoonful of salt, and white pepper to taste. Beat until very light and then add the well-beaten whites of two eggs. Stir in gradually. Fill the skins with this mixture, brush over with yolks of the eggs and place in the oven until brown, about fifteen minutes.

*

Swiss Style Eggs

Cover the bottom of a dish with two ounces of butter, and on this scatter grated cheese. Drop the eggs upon the cheese without breaking the yolks. Season to taste. Pour over the eggs a little cream and sprinkle with about two ounce of grated cheese. Set in moderate oven for about fifteen minutes.

*

Sweet Potato Croquettes

Peel and mash smooth three or four medium sized potatoes, beat into them one tablespoon butter, one teaspoon salt, and one lightly beaten egg. If too dry, add boiling milk. Beat well and shape into croquettes. Dip in beaten egg and roll in bread or cracker crumbs. Fry in hot lard until a rich brown. Serve at once.

*

Asparagus with Eggs

Boil asparagus until tender, then place in a baking dish; season well. Beat the yolks of four eggs light, add two tablespoonfuls of cream, and two level tablepoonfuls of butter, salt and pepper and the whites of the eggs, beaten to a froth. Pour over the asparagus; set in the oven and bake until the eggs are set.

*

Roast Turkey

Rub thoroughly inside and out with salt and pepper. Fill with dressing made as follows: One loaf stale bread, crumbed and moistened with boiling water. Season with pepper, salt and sage to taste. Add one-half pound of butter, cut into bits, and one quart raw oysters, being careful not to break them. Stuff the breast first. Sew up both openings and tie the neck down upon the breast. Lay the points of the wings under the back and tie in place with twine. Press the legs closely towards the breast and side-bones as possible and fasten with twine. Tie the ends of the legs to the tail. Place in dripping pan with a little water and butter. Spread the turkey with butter, salt and pepper. In roasting, allow twenty minutes time for each pound and twenty minutes longer. Baste often and turn until nicely browned on all sides.

*

Roast Beef

The second cut of the rib and the sirloin are considered the choice cuts. Allow fifteen minutes to every pound, or twenty, if liked well done. Place in dripping pan with piece of suet. Put no water in pan, nor salt on meat. Baste frequently with the fat in pan. Have your oven hot when you put your meat in and let it gradually get cooler. Dish meat and pour off all fat, for greasy gravies are bad for the stomach and the complexion, too. Add boiling water according to the quantity of gravy desired. Stir in flour mixed smoothly with a little water. Do not make too thick. Season meat and gravy with salt and pepper to taste.

*

Yorkshire Pudding with Roast Beef

Three cups of flour, half teaspoon salt, two teaspoons baking powder, one large tablespoon butter. Rub butter into the flour; then stir in two beaten eggs and one-half cup milk. Should be a thick batter. Turn into pan with roast and bake twenty minutes.

*

Two Fathers At Christmas

By Mark Nixon

The country was in a recession the Christmas of 1959, I was told years later.

"Jobs are scarcer than good venison," said a neighbor, and people weighed their words solemnly. The summer people had long since fled to the cities, packing into their station wagons and campers our community's livelihood. Even the deer hunters had departed, their convoys rumbling out of town on the south-bound highway as noisily as they had rumbled in.

Our town lay hushed and forgotten. Those fortunate few with jobs that did not vanish along with the city tourists were envied secretly. Others cut pulp wood for as long as their backs held out. A few found work pumping gas or driving fuel oil trucks. All the while, the fiercest winter in recent memory howled at our doors.

I was ten, with more serious matters in mind. The dreadful discovery was upon me: my childhood Christmases were over. All belief in things magical and wondrous were cast away. Christmas was a lifeless seasonal oddity, sapped by my own loss of innocence. It was a shadow, and I dwelled in the heart of it. It was more than a young soul could bear.

A week before Christmas, I tried to pry myself out of this sorry state. "Giving is better than receiving" was a line uttered a few million times throughout my school days, and while I never gave it much thought before, the notion now seized me with a will of its own.

I set off for town, determined to buy my family the best Christmas possible — for nine dollars and some odd change. Walking briskly from store to store, I quickly bought socks and handkerchiefs for my father, a scarf and a candy dish for my mother, plastic dolls for my little sisters.

My other brother's gift was the last on the list. My older brother — the one I worshipped. Marching into the hardware store, I dipped into my pocket and retrieved the last of my savings. Twenty-one cents. The man behind the counter was eager to sell me anything. It took little to convince me that a spool of fishing line was a fine gift for an older brother.

I slunk out of the store, tears burning my cheeks. My father found me on the street corner, and through the sobs I told him what had happened. Wordlessly he grasped my hand and led me back to the store. Locating an ice fishing tip-up my brother so wanted, he brusquely paid for it and fairly stomped out of the store.

It was a side of my father I had never seen. I cannot be sure what was on his mind at that moment, though I've wondered about it from time to time. It may have been his way of telling the world, "My children will not be denied a Christmas." He was not a boastful man, nor one to accept charity. He was immensely proud of his ability to muddle through. Times like the winter of '59 must have pained him: to work into the wee hours delivering fuel oil, rarely seeing his family; giving a Christmas to his children that was not all he wanted it to be.

Though my hurt and embarrassment did not completely dissolve that wintry afternoon, I never loved my father more than the moment he stalked out of the hardware store, prideful and defiant.

I stood outside our home late that Christmas Eve, in a stillness only a northern Michigan winter can conjure. The air was so crisp it hurt to breathe.

Late Christmas Eve, and I saw this: a midnight sky swaddled in a wreath of stars. They quivered in expectation, seeming entirely reachable beyond the boughs of the white pines. I felt the whole universe eying my every step.

Snow crackling under my rubber boots echoed in the woods beyond. I scudded through a fresh drift and felt the sting on my ankles when a few crystals sneaked over the boot tops.

I heard this: my mother in the kitchen rolling out the last pastry shell for the last mincemeat pie; my sisters begging for a final piece of datenut roll. Whatever else leaner times thrust upon us, our mother made certain the pies and sweets never deserted us.

We were bound for midnight Mass, normally a joyless affair. I wore a 95-cent clip-on tie, and my only suit, a navy blue nightmare that fit like a straight jacket.

Soon we trudged off to church. My father, reared in another religion, remained at home. We left him sitting in a shadowy spot beside the lighted Christmas tree, where he read from my grandmother's Bible. It was a strange comfort to me, when we returned home hours later, that I would find him guarding our quiet home, Bible drooping in hands and fast asleep.

The priest that night was a stranger, as most priests were to our church in Harrison. We were a mission church, and played host to a parade of visiting priests of the Dominican and Franciscan Orders.

His name was Father John McCabe. He was endowed with a ponderous girth; an aging giant of a man in flowing white vestments. He might have been typecast to play the role of Friar Tuck, had it not been for his eyes. They were rivets of cold steel, stern and heartless looking. He might have smashed the pulpit with his looks alone, if not with his sheer bulk. Turning from the altar, his eyes swept over the congregation with a look that awakened new fears in those who dared look back.

He stroke to the pulpit and then gingerly — almost daintily — he ascended. Never since have I witnessed such a complete and instantaneous transformation. The hellfire and brimstone look vanished, and there before us stood a bemused, comically oversized angel draped in white. I squirmed in anticipation.

He chuckled loudly over the coughs and foot shuffles. "Oh, the splendid dinner I had tonight," he began. His meal was, of course, many hours past, in accordance with the Church's fasting laws. But his memory of it, to the last morsel, was so vivid that it was almost sinful.

He closed his eyes and feasted again. I closed mine and dined with him; the second helping of turkey and dressing, the bite of fresh cranberry sauce, the candied yams and corn and dills and three kinds of pies for dessert. It was a feast, yes, and a joyous one.

Father McCabe ended his all-too-brief sermon with these words: "My good friends, have a wonderful Christmas feast, for today we celebrate the joy of Life." What more could he possibly say to a ten-year-old boy about a carpenter's son born 1,949 years before me?

Christmas was hours old when I discarded my ill-fitting church clothes, burrowed deep under blankets and tumbled into long sleep. At dawn, presents were unwrapped with unmerciful haste. The rest of the day plodded. Nothing is so empty as the waning moments of Christmas.

Yet the memory of two fathers lingered, made itself felt in later years. Both domineering and gruff in appearance, both secreting reservoirs of compassion. One proud and barely restraining his anger, the other bold enough to laugh out loud in church, in joy.

The door to my childhood Christmases had closed forever, but thanks to two older and wiser men, a spark of boyish joy come Christmas has never dimmed.

Selection of Choice Receipts,

St. Paul's Guild of the Episcopal Church of Lansing

Angels Food

Eleven eggs, whites only, one and a half tumblers of granulated sugar, one tumbler of flour, one teaspoon of vanilla, one teaspoon of cream of tartar. Sift the flour four times, then add the cream of tartar and sift again, but have the right measure before putting in the cream of tartar. Sift the sugar and measure. Beat the eggs to a stiff froth on a large platter; on the same platter add the sugar very lightly, then the flour very gently, then the vanilla; do not stop beating until you put it in the pan to bake. Bake it forty minutes in a very moderate oven. Try with a straw and if too soft let it remain a few minutes longer. Turn the pan upside down to cool, and when cold take out by loosening around the sides with a knife. Use a pan that has never been greased, and will allow a space between the pan and the table when it is turned upside down. The tumbler for measuring must hold two and one-quarter gills.

*

Fruit Cake

Ten pounds stoned raisins, two pounds of citron, one and a quarter pounds of flour, one pound of butter washed free from salt, one pound dark brown sugar, one dozen eggs, half pint of molasses, two-thirds of a pint of good brandy, half a pint of sweet cream, two ounces of cinnamon, one ounce of cloves, one ounce of mace, one ounce of allspice, one nutmeg, the rinds of three lemons grated fine. If you do not wish the trouble of stoning so many raisins, you can put in two or three pounds of English currants in place of the same quantity of raisins. If you use all raisins, a pound and a half of flour will not be too much.

Mix all the fruits, currants, raisins and citron thoroughly. Then sift in the flour and rub through the fruit. Put your butter and sugar into your cake bowl and rub them thoroughly together to a cream; separate your eggs, put the yolks into the butter and sugar and stir them thoroughly together, then add spices, molasses, cream, grated lemon peel, then stir in your fruit and flour by handsful thoroughly through it all. Whip the whites of the eggs stiff, then stir your brandy into the cake, and last of all the whites of the eggs.

The following is a good recipe for lining your tins to prevent drying and burning of the fruit cake:

Grease the tins with lard, line them with heavy brown paper, make a thick flour paste that will spread, spread it on the brown paper, then add another lining of brown paper on the paste, grease the brown paper, then put a thickness of white tea paper over that and grease it also.

*

Currant Pie

One cup of mashed currants, one cup of sugar, one cup of water, two tablespoons of flour, the yolks of two eggs, using the whites for frosting. Bake with one crust.

*

Lemon Pie

One cup of boiling water, one cup of sugar, one tablespoon of corn starch, yolks of three eggs, grated rind and juice of one large lemon. Cook in a farina kettle. Bake the crust, then fill with the custard and add the beaten whites. Return to the oven to brown.

*

A fragrant and always with you disinfectant — scatter ground cinnamon slowly on a shovelful of hot coals.

Soft Gingerbread

One cup of sugar, one cup of molasses, one cup of sour milk, half a cup of butter and lard mixed, two eggs, two teaspoonsful of soda dissolved in the milk. Ginger, cinnamon and cloves to taste, three cups of flour. Bake in a moderate oven.

*

Vanilla Sauce

Cook one pint of sweet milk, one tablespoon of cornstarch, beaten yolks of three eggs, half a cup of sugar. Flavor with vanilla.

*

Ginger Snaps

One cup of molasses, one cup of granulated sugar, one cup of butter, two eggs well beaten, one teaspoonful of ginger, one teaspoonful of soda dissolved in a tablespoonful of vinegar. Let the molasses, sugar and butter come to a boil, then cool before mixing with the others. Mix and bake.

*

Cranberry Shortcake

Prepare a light delicate cake as for strawberry shortcake. Spread plentifully with melted butter to make it rich. To three pints of cranberries add three and a half cups of sugar and stew with sufficient water to make a stiff jelly. When partly cool, spread the cake with a thick layer of the cranberries. Sprinkle with sugar and grate nutmeg over them, and put together.

*

Coffee Cake Without Eggs

Three-fourths of a cup of butter, one cup of brown sugar, one cup of New Orleans molasses, one cup of strong cold coffee, one teaspoonful of soda in the molasses, one-half teaspoonful in the coffee, one nutmeg, two tablespoonsful of ground cinnamon, one of cloves, one cup of seeded raisins, flour enough to make a stiff batter. Bake.

*

German Cookies

One pound of brown sugar, half a cup of lard, one teaspoon of salt, one quart of molasses, one pint of sour cream, quarter of a pound of citron, quarter of a pound of almonds. Chop citron and almonds. Add one ounce of cloves, one ounce of cinnamon, one nutmeg, three-fourth of a tablespoon of soda. Mix and bake as any cookies

*

Red Raspberry Shrub

To one quart of berries, add one pint of vinegar, let stand twenty-four hours, then add one pound of sugar to every pint of juice, boil twenty minutes, then bottle.

*

Coffee

One large tablespoon of coffee, and a cup of boiling water for each person. Mix the coffee with an egg and a little cold water, then pour on the boiling water and let it boil fifteen minutes, pour in a little cold water, and let stand two or three minutes on the back of the range to settle. If one cannot have cream, the white of an egg whipped stiff and added to the milk is an improvement upon milk alone. It should be put in the cup with the sugar before the coffee is poured in.

*

Chocolate

One square of Baker's chocolate, add an equal quantity of sugar and mix with a little boiling water. Add to this one pint of boiling milk, let boil five minutes. A tablespoon of whipped cream flavored with vanilla and sweetened and laid on the top of the cups improves it. It should be served immediately.

*

Pickled Cherries

To seven pounds of pitted cherries, take one pint of vinegar and one and one-half pounds brown sugar. Boil the vinegar and sugar and put in little bags of whole cloves and stick cinnamon. Pour this boiling liquid over the uncooked cherries, which should be in a stone crock. Leave the little bags of spices also in. For five consecutive days, drain off the liquor and scald it and pour over the cherries. One the sixth day boil the cherries with the juice and bottle at once.

*

Cheese Straws

One cup of grated cheese and one tablespoon butter creamed together, four tablespoons of cold water, a dust of cayenne pepper and salt, enough flour to roll out, cut into strips and bake to a delicate brown.

*

Cranberry Jelly

One quart of cranberries, one cup of water; boil fifteen minutes in a graniteware or earthen saucepan, and then rub through a sieve. Return to fire with one pint of granulated sugar, boil five minutes and pour into molds.

*

Tomato Preserves

Nine pounds tomatoes, seven pounds of sugar, two pounds of figs, two or three lemons sliced, cook at least two hours. This is nice used as filling for cake.

*

Scalloped Corn

To one can of corn, add one tablespoon of flour, one well-beaten egg, three tablespoons of melted butter, salt, pepper and half a teacup of milk. Bake to a light brown.

*

Escalloped Potatoes

Pare and slice thin potatoes enough to fill a pint basin; in the bottom of the basin put a layer of potatoes, adding salt, then another layer and salt, and so on till the basin is almost full. Then fill the basin with sweet cream, set in the oven, and bake forty minutes, or until the potatoes are a pale lemon yellow on top and soft clear through. If cream cannot be had, use sweet milk and a little butter. This is enough for six people for tea, and is very nice with cold ham or tongue.

*

Spinach a la Creme

Boil spinach until tender; chop very fine; rub through a colander; season with salt, pepper and a little grated nutmeg. Put in a saucepan; stir over the fire until warm, pour in three tablespoonsful of cream; add a quarter of a pound of butter and a teaspoonful of sugar. Stir it over the fire for five minutes, and serve it piled high in the center of the dish, or pressed into a form, garnished with boiled eggs.

*

Young Beets

Boil beets in hot water one hour; when done, rub off the skins; split the beets lengthwise and lay upon a hot dish; have ready a great spoonful of melted butter mixed with two of vinegar, a little salt and pepper, heated to boiling and pour over the beets.

*

Scalloped Tomatoes

Peel and cut tomatoes in slices quarter of an inch thick. Pack in a pudding dish in alternate layers, with a force-meat made of bread crumbs, butter, salt, pepper and a little white sugar. Spread thickly upon each stratum of tomatoes, and when the dish is nearly full, put tomatoes uppermost, a good bit of butter upon each slice. Dust with pepper and a little sugar. Strew with dry bread crumbs and bake covered, half an hour. Remove the lid and bake brown.

*

Tomato Soup

One quart of soup stock, one quart of tomatoes, one cup butter, one quart sweet milk, one and a half cups of flour. Put the stock and tomatoes to boil one hour, then strain, cream the flour and butter, and pour into the soup, add the milk boiling the last thing. Then remove from the fire, salt to taste.

*

Turkey Dressed with Oysters

Wash the turkey outside and inside very clean. Take bread crumbs, grated or chopped, about enough to fill the turkey, with butter the size of a large egg, pepper, salt and sweet herbs to your taste. Then work in a well-beaten egg. Fill the crop and body with alternate layers of dressing and well-drained oysters. Turkey must be cooked very thoroughly.

*

Dressing for Turkey

For a turkey weighing ten pounds, use two small loaves of soft bread, laying aside the crust. Tear the loaves apart, and either chop them or grate them on a coarse grater. Then add one egg well-beaten, a teaspoonful of pepper, a teaspoonful of salt, one-half teaspoon of sage, and one-half teaspoon of summer savory. Drop in small bits, nearly one-half cup of butter, and mix lightly with the hand. Garnish with fried oysters.

*

The Eve of Epiphany:
(Legends of Le Detroit), 1884

By Marie Caroline Watson Hamlin

The visitor to Detroit's Hotel de Ville will notice on either side of the main entrance two "long nines" mounted on stone carriages. These grim sentinels are the trophies of the great "Battle of Lake Erie." The proud Mistress of the Seas for the first time in her history was forced to surrender an entire fleet, and to children whose grandsires she had cradled. Young America points to these cannons with pride and a glow of patriotism steals into his heart as he reads the thrilling account of the battle. The grey-haired Octogenarian tenderly pats the guns and recalls memories of days that have gone, social pleasures, friends of his youth and beauty mouldering in the grave.

In 1801, some years before the outbreak of hostilities with England, the habitants of these "Cotes" had, with returning prosperity, resumed much of their old time gaiety. In winter, the exciting races on the ice between the swift French ponies; in the spring the annual crop of weddings with the long procession of charrettes (French carts) laden with a joyous, light-hearted freight of gay girls; and in autumn the corn huskings were again in vogue. Each feast day of the church had its peculiar and appropriate customs handed down from their Norman ancestry.

It was on the eve of one of these, the Epiphany, that in a hospitable old mansion on the present site of Windsor, was assembled a brilliant party of stately dames, fair demoiselles and courtly cavaliers, mingled with the elite of the young Scot element. There seemed to be some latent chord of sympathy between these brave Highlanders and the French, for intermarriages were of frequent occurrence.

The table was laid for supper, which was to be followed by games, fortune telling, etc. Seated near the head of the table, between two dashing gallants who had vied with each other for her bright glances, was a young Kentucky widow on a visit to the settlement. Her husband had been killed a few years previous in one of the Indian raids, leaving her with a merry little boy to soothe her grief.

The large Epiphany cake was cut by the host, each lady present taking a piece. It was then customary to put in it a ring and a small white bean. The lady to whose lot the ring fell was crowned queen. The holder of the bean gave the entertainment the following year, and acted on the present occasion, as maid of honor. Madame Fairbairne found the ring and Julie Maisonville the bean. It was then necessary for the fortunate queen to select the king of Epiphany.

Madame Fairbairne blushed as her eyes wandered from one to the other of her two gallants, and she said, "If we choose Monsieur Grant, we shall offend Monsieur Brevoort, if we choose Monsieur Brevoort we shall offend Monsieur Grant. We shall select the one who is to become the most distinguished, and to ascertain this we decree that our noble Dame D'Honneur, Mlle. Maisonville, shall take the grounds from the pot of tea and tell the fortune of all three of us. You know that she is a witch herself and in league with all the witches, so it is our royal pleasure that she shall explain to us what say the fates, and to their decree we must bow."

A murmur of assent greeted the queen's proposition, and a large platter being brought Mlle. Julie, with many incantations in a wild jumble of words learned from the Indian magicians, turned the contents of the teapot out onto the platter, where the leaves assumed strange and wild forms that only the initiated could read.

In those days, clairvoyance and mind reading were but little known, and there was more of a disposition to impute effects to supernatural than to natural causes. Witchcraft was the name then given to moder spiritualism. Fortune telling was frequently and devoutly believed in, expecially when the person was the seventh daughter of a seventh daughter. In those times of a plethora of children, this was no uncommon thing. Julie was the mystic seventh daughter, and she was noted throughout the colony for her wonderful powers of divination. Whilst her beauty was of a seductive, fascinating order, there seemed at times to be something beyond human ken in her lustrous eye. Though universally beloved, there were many who looked with awe on her mysterious powers.

After eagerly scanning the tea grounds, she closed her eyes a moment as if communing with herself, and heaving a deep sigh said in a chanting tone to her profoundly interested audience: "My friends, I see here wonderful things. On this holy night of Epiphany when three wise men came from the East and learned the secrets of the future, it is fitting that I, the humble maid of our gracious queen, should reveal to you at her bidding what fate has ordained.

"This line," pointing toward the platter, "represents Monsieur Brevoort, and this Monsieur Grant, whilst this one describes the fate of our noble queen. These two young men are destined to wonderful careers. Today they are intimate friends. Later you will see them contending with one another, but not alone. A great war is indicated, accompanied by terrible bloodshed. The contest between these two seems to be on the water, the victory for a time is evenly balanced, but later it seems to belong to you, Monsieur Brevoort. Your line of life is not ended, Monsieur Grant. You will both settle down by the lakes around happy fireplaces."

ꙅ ꙅ

Suddenly the prophetess turned deadly pale as she scanned more critically the tea grounds.

"I see here by your line, honored queen, the figure of a tomahawk; great trouble will come to you through the Indians. A little off-shoot of your line seems to cross that of Monsieur Grant, and ends with many branches. This, gracious queen, is all I see in the shadowy future."

The queen then addressed her loyal subjects as follows: "My children, the words of the sibyl indeed perplex me. I am compelled to decide for myself. Although Monsieur Brevoort seems to carry off the palm of victory, yet my line seems to cross that of Monsieur Grant. My ambition prompts me to select Monsieur Brevoort as my king, but fate seems to point in another direction.

"On two such charming cavaliers I would not bring the trouble that is in store for me. It is evident I need a strong arm to protect me, a king with an army at his back. I therefore choose as king of Epiphany (here her eyes fell upon Col. Brush standing near the door) the gallant Colonel of the Legionary Corps. His veterans will never suffer harm to come to their queen."

At this, Col. Brush came forward and was crowned king. The company, charmed with the graceful manner of the young widow, applauded her choice. The festivites were kept up to a late hour, but the union of the king and queen extended no further than Epiphany's eve. She soon returned with her little son to her home on the Kentucky border.

As the inspired Franklin had said years before, "The war of the Revolution has been fought, the war of Independence has still to be fought." The long smouldering element at last burst its bonds. Detroit disgracefully surrendered at the first onset. An English fleet built on the river, controlled the lakes, but the dying words of the heroic Lawrence were impressed on the American minds: "Don't give up the ship."

Under the direction of the daring young Rhode Islander, Oliver Hazard Perry, a fleet was hastily constructed at Presque Isle on the south shore of Lake Erie. On the 10 of September, 1813, from his look-out on Gibraltar Island, Put-in-Bay, Perry discovered the British fleet sailing out of the Detroit River to attack him. It was composed of six vessels carrying seventy guns. The Americans had nine vessels carrying fifty-four guns. In weight of metal and efficiency, the British fleet seemed superior and its commander, Barclay, was one of Nelson's veterans. Young Perry flung out his ensign with the legend, "Don't give up the ship," and was determined that day to conquer or die. When twilight had set in that night, American valor had enabled him to write this immortal dispatch from his ship moored off one of the Three Sisters Islands. "We have met the enemy, and they are ours — two ships, two brigs, one schooner, one sloop." This was the decisive blow of the war. Harrison soon afterwards drove the cowardly Proctor from Detroit and unfurled again the starry flag, where long may it wave.

In command of the marines on the American fleet was Lt. Henry Brevoort, of the 3rd regiment of U.S. Infantry detailed for duty on the fleet. Later he was known as Commodore Brevoort. Congress voted him a medal for his gallantry and his grateful country will ever cherish his memory. Commodore Alexander Grant commanded one of the British vessels in the action. He married Miss Barthe at Detroit and after the war built his residence, called "Grant's Castle," at Grosse Pointe, where it was the scene of much hospitality.

Shortly after one of the Indian raids into Ohio and Kentucky, Mrs. Grant heard that a band of savages had encamped at Belle Isle. They were going to hold a pow wow to celebrate their exploits, and to torture and burn a young white captive whose mother they had killed.

The Commodore was away, but his wife's motherly instincts were roused, and knowing the love and esteem of the Indians for her family, she determined to make an effort to save the poor boy from so terrible a fate.

She was rowed to Belle Isle, made her way to the camp and asked the amount of the ransom for the child. The Indians, who were making preparations for their horrible feast, would not at

first listen to her. The courageous woman was not to be baffled, and at last partly by lavish presents and partly by threats that the black gown (priest) would bring some calamity on them, she succeeded in her mission.

The little boy was brought home and adopted by his humane deliverer, who already had a large family (ten daughters) of her own.

On the Commodore's return, his good wife described to him her visit to the Indian encampment and its gratifying results.

"What did the Indians call him?" suddenly exclaimed the Commodore.

"I think they called him fair bairn or pretty boy," she replied.

The old veteran bowed his head, whilst memory was busy weaving the broken links of the prophecy on Epiphany eve, many years before.

The Bessemer Cookery,

The Presbyterian Ladies Aid, 1929

Frozen Fruit Salad

1 can pineapple
1 can white cherries
1 can pears
2 oranges
Juice of one lemon
$1/4$ grapefruit
1 pt. mayonnaise
1 pt. cream, whipped

Cut fruit size of half cherry. Mix fruit juice, mayonnaise and cream. Pour into can of a freezer and turn crank slowly until frozen. Pack frozen mixture into quart molds. Let stand one-half to one hour. Slice and serve slices on lettuce hearts with French dressing made with lemon juice. Recipe serves 30.

*

Pineapple and Date Salad

$^{1}/_{2}$ lb. dates
1 can sliced pineapple
$^{1}/_{2}$ c. white cherries of Malaga grapes
$^{1}/_{4}$ c. chopped pecans
Whipped cream

Chop fruit, except pineapple, and nuts. Place slices of pineapple on lettuce leaves. Spread fruit mixed with whipped cream on pineapple. Place nut or cherry in center of pineapples.

*

Christmas Salad

One slice of red pineapple, cover with cream cheese, then place another slice of white pineapple on cheese. Chill one hour, divide in half and cut in wedge shape. Top with mayonnaise and red cherries. Serve with lettuce leaf on plate.

*

Butterfly Salad

Arrange lettuce leaves on a salad plate. Cut a slice of pineapple and place on the lettuce leaf with rounded edges together. This will be the wings of the butterfly. Slice a banana in half lengthwise and place between the rounded edges of the pineapple. This represents the body. For eyes, put in tiny bits of raisins. Cut narrow strips of pimento for the antenna. The decorations on the wings may be represented by finely cut nuts and coconut sprinkled over them.

*

Sweet Potato Balls

6 sweet potatoes, boiled, mashed
Salt and pepper
Cornflakes
3 tablespoons margarine
8 marshmallows
2 tablespoons cream

Add margarine to mashed potatoes and stir in cream. With hand, form into balls, pressing marshmallow in the center. Roll in cornflakes and reheat in a dish by placing in oven until ready to serve.

*

Sweet Potato Pone

5 medium sized sweet potatoes
$^1/_2$ c. seedless raisins
$^1/_2$ c. sugar
1 tablespoon butter
1/8 teaspoon nutmeg
$^1/_2$ cup condensed milk
Peel and slice the potatoes, add raisins, cook until the potatoes are tender. Drain, add the sugar, butter and nutmeg and beat until creamy. Add the milk, place in a buttered baking dish and bake in a moderate oven until golden bropwn. Before serving, place marshmallows on top and return to oven to brown.

*

Glazed Sweet Potatoes

Pare and boil sweet potatoes for 10 minutes in salted water. Drain, slice and arrange in buttered baking dish. Cover liberally with a mixture of brown sugar and butter. Add enough of water that potatoes have been boiled in to almost cover potatoes. Bake slowly till potatoes are well saturated with carmel.

*

Grand Rapid Receipt Book,

Ladies of the Congregational Church, 1873

Bavarian Cream

1 pt. cream sweetened very sweet, 3 tablespoons wine, 1 tablespoon vanilla; after beating the cream up lightly, stir in 1/3 of a box of "Cox's Sparkling Gelatine" dissolved in 1/2 teacup of warm water; while straining in the gelatine beat the cream thoroughly, add the whites of 6 eggs well beaten; beat them all together, pour into a mould and let it stand an hour in a cool place; serve with or without jelly.

*

Speaking tubes are cheap, and save a lot of running (and hollering) up and down stairs.

Molasses Candy

2 cups molasses, 1 cup sugar, 1 tablespoon vinegar, butter size of a nut, $1/2$ teaspoon soda; boil briskly 20 minutes stirring all the time, when cool enough pull quickly.

*

Boston Brown Bread

2 cups Indian meal, 1 cup rye meal (mixed thoroughly), $2/3$ cup molasses, 1 cake "Twin Brothers" yeast or $2/3$ cup home-brewed yeast, 1 teaspoon soda, mix with warm water, very stiff, a little salt. Butter thoroughly a pail (a 3-quart tin pail) and put in the bread; fasten the pail in a pot of boiling water, and let the bread steam in this way 5 hours or longer.

*

Tree-mendous: Michigan's Christmas Trees

By Judith Eldridge

The Christmas tree; breathing its piney fragrance through the house, its winking lights reflected in the tinsel and treasures hanging from the boughs, a star or angel or other family keepsake topping it all! Without the tree, no amount of Santa Clauses, or carols from every corner, holly wreaths or bells, or secrets carefully kept since way before Thanksgiving, can make Christmas complete.

The tradition of the tree is younger than St. Nicholas, the giving of gifts and even caroling, but except for the Holy Creche, no symbol of Christmas seems so important to the keeping of the season. Why else would families, as some have been known to do, keep the tree up long after the season, waiting for some absent member to return?

So, while we admit that some people do get through Christmas without having a tree, most of us do not. And "getting the tree" is almost as important a ritual as decorating it.

The questions is, what kind of a tree?

Michigan shoppers have more trees to choose from than in any other state. We grow more than a fourth of all the Christmas trees harvested commercially in the country, and while the majority of them are shipped out of state — Florida is a big buyer of Michigan trees — there are plenty left for us to choose from.

Scotch pine is the most popular, both for buyers and growers (about 80 percent of Michigan's plantation-grown trees are Scotch pine). They grow quickly and evenly, and buyers like them because they are full and hold their needles well.

Douglas fir and balsam have a heavier evergreen fragrance, and cost more.

Spruce and cedar are second most popular; spruce cost less but die too quickly.

Christmas trees are a crop, and the 900 or so commercial growers in Michigan harvest six or seven million trees annually for the 21 million households in the United States that will be putting up a real tree. Some of the western states — Oregon, for instance — harvest mountain-grown trees.

A lot of people like to go out and cut down their tree themselves. And if you don't have your own woods with evergreen trees in it, there are about 75 cut-your-own tree farms around the state (you can't just go out in any woods and cut down trees).

You can get a list of these tree farms from the State Department of Agriculture or the Michigan Christmas Tree Association.

Don't think that whether you buy it off the lot or cut it yourself you'll be getting this year's most perfect tree. That goes to the governor's office. Each year, the Michigan Christmas Tree Association holds a competition, with the winning tree going to the governor. (It would be too big for your living roon, anyway.) The national association holds a competition, too, with state winners competing. That tree goes to the White House. It was not just coincidence that one of the years Gerald Ford was president, the national winner came from Michigan; he put in a word that he'd like a tree from his home state.

There are some things to remember when choosing your tree. It will look smaller on the lot or in the field than it will in your house. Judge its height by your own, and allow a little extra for the height of the stand and room for an ornament on top.

Do you really need a perfect tree? If it's going to stand in a corner or next to the wall, you can buy one with an imperfect side and put that to the back.

If you have lots of ornaments, you can get by with a tree with a few skimpy spots, and it might cost less, and fill them in when you decorate it. But if you're shy on ornaments, better get a full one with no holes.

Most important is to get one with a straight trunk. Almost any other imperfection can be overcome (only God can make a tree, but He doesn't guarantee they'll all be perfect) but a crooked trunk means a lop-sided tree, no matter what you do to it.

In some families, dad goes out to buy the tree. In some, everybody does. Some families save the tree-trimming for Christmas Eve; some have their tree up the day after Thanksgiving. Martin Luther is said to have cut down the first Christmas tree and decorated it with candles to signify the starry skies of Bethlehem the night Christ was born. However, "having a tree" got its start in the English-speaking world when Queen Victoria put up a tree at Windsor Castle about 1844. It has gained in popularity ever since, although it was not until the late 1800s that it became popular in the United States (the Pilgrims didn't even celebrate Christmas; it was just another work day to them).

Whatever family tradition you use, and whether you get your tree from the lot down the street or go out and cut your own, there are some things to remember. Here's a checklist to take with you:

The base of the tree should be about two-thirds of the height; that is, if you get a seven-foot tree, the base should be about four feet across.

Make sure the trunk will fit your tree stand. And make sure your stand will support the size tree you get.

Check the height, the symmetry and the fullness, and get a tree that will fill your needs.

If you buy your tree at a lot, check the trunk; it should be sticky at the cut. If it's not, the tree has been cut too long and has dried out already. Pick another one.

Shake it; if more than a few needles fall off, put it back and get another one, that one's too dry.

When you get your tree home, slice about half an inch off the bottom and stand the tree in a bucket of water. Check your stand and make sure it holds water, about a gallon. Once you get your tree up, water it every day.

Keep your tree away from heaters, registers and radiators, stoves, fireplaces and candles. They will hasten the drying, for one thing, and that will create a fire hazard.

Check your light strings, too, before you put them on the tree; a broken wire could mean a short and that could mean a fire.

As with everything else, prices are probably going to be higher this year than last. But who counts cost with something so important as the Christmas tree. So get out the boxes of decorations saved from Christmases past.

INDEX

Relishes, Sauces, Etc

Salads

Breads

Beverages

Cookies and Candy

129

Dolls have always been a traditional Christmas toy. This one is from the Michigan History Museum in Lansing.

For information on other Eberly Press books, write to:

eberly press

1004 Michigan Ave.
E. Lansing, MI 48823

About the Author

Carole Eberly is a former legislative reporter for United Press International. A freelance writer and editor, she is also a faculty member at Michigan State University's School of Journalism. Besides cooking and eating, Carole's pasttimes include running, going to the movies, playing with her five cats, finding great bargains at various stores and lazing around a log cabin (with a great fireplace and no telephone) in Northern Michigan. This is Carole's eleventh cookbook.